WAS HE A PERFECT GENTLEMAN?

'A CLASSIC WHODUNNIT'

PAT BACKLEY

CONTENTS

ACKNOWLEDGEMENTS

As always I dedicate this book to my beloved daughter Lucy. Without your love and support I would have struggled over the last few years.

What inspired me to write a whodunnit?
It is a little different from my usual genres!

The idea came to me after attending a talk at my local library. Four crime writers were talking about their books and the next morning I woke up with almost the entire plot for this book in my head.

I have met so many fabulous people over the course of my life and many of you feature in some small way in this book. Not as whole characters, rest assured none of you are the murderer!
But so much inspiration has come from my memories of the past, from people, places and events.

I do hope you enjoy this story.

1

APRIL 1986, EASTBOURNE, SUSSEX,
ENGLAND

Betty had often wondered if he was quite as perfect as he seemed.

She had hardly ever spoken to him of course, just the odd hello as they passed on the street, but her mum had always referred to him as *that nice Mr. Jones, a perfect gentleman.* Betty had never spent enough time with him to know if that was true.

And now she would never know for sure.

The only thing she did know was that he was now *perfectly dead,* his frozen body lying beneath a fresh coating of snow.

Her screams echoed around the lane. They were so loud that it woke the neighbours. Lights were switched on in the surrounding houses, illuminating the dark alleyway.

IT TOOK the police ten minutes to arrive at the scene. It had been a quiet night and when the emergency call came in they had all been sitting around the police station gas fire, enjoying mugs of steaming hot chocolate.

Two uniformed officers got out of the squad car; Fred who was nearing retirement and his young sidekick Andy, a fresh faced lad straight from police training college. By now there was quite a crowd in the lane.

"Ok then, so what do we have here?"

It was a rather silly question. It was pretty obvious that what they had here was a dead body. A body that must have been there all night, judging by the fact that until Betty had kicked it with her foot, it had been completely covered with fresh snow.

Fred, the older of the two policeman took control of the situation.

"Now then, let's calm down everybody. I know it's been an awful shock for you all, but could you please return to your homes now. We'll be doing a door to door search later, talking to all of you. But now we need to clear the lane, so the ambulance can get through."

Eventually the ambulance arrived and the body was taken to the morgue at the local hospital. The two police officers hung around, taking notes. They had called for a female officer to go with them to break the bad news to Mrs. Jones. There were no lights coming from number 47, so it seemed that she was probably still fast asleep, quite unaware of the fact that she was now a widow.

THE AMBULANCE MAN had gently brushed away some of the snow covering the body, exposing a tall, slim man, about six feet tall, with a rather handsome face. His bushy eyebrows and moustache, still with their covering of pristine white snow, made him look like an old man.

"HE LIVES at number 47 with his wife Vera. Has anyone told her yet?"

"I EXPECT HE WAS DRUNK. He often staggered home after spending all evening in the pub. Bit of a drinker he was you know, officer."

"STILL, what an awful way to die, freezing to death outside all night. Outside his own home. Gives you the shivers."

"I GUESS someone will have to let the bank know. They'll need to get a temporary manager in I suppose."

"WELL, I can't say I'm sorry. He was a miserable old bugger, always yelling at my kids when their ball went over his fence. I do feel for his wife though, lovely woman Vera is. I never thought he deserved her."

•   •   •

"Poor Betty, what a shock to find his body lying there. She'll have nightmares for weeks about that."

"Andy, can you please go and take a statement from the young lady who found him. Betty her name is and she lives right there." Fred pointed to the back gate opposite to where the body had been discovered.

Ten minutes later, Andy found himself sitting at a pine kitchen table, drinking tea from an enormous blue mug. The young woman sitting opposite him looked very pale and had obviously been crying.

"I'm so sorry Miss, I know it's been an awful shock for you, finding the body like that, but I do need to take a statement from you."

She sniffed and wiped a stray tear that was running down her cheek. Even in her extreme distress he could see that she was a very pretty girl. Only about his age he reckoned.

"So, Miss, I just need your full name, age and address please."

"Oh I'm not Miss, I'm married. My husband is called Ian and we live here with my mum and dad at the moment. Oh and I'm 23 years old, 24 next birthday."

She took off her thick woollen gloves and he noticed the gold ring on her wedding finger.

· · ·

HE REALISED that she was still in shock and very nervous, so rather than ask any more questions, he just let her speak in her own time.

"I WAS REALLY surprised to see the garden covered in snow. Although it was a bit cold last night, no-one, not even the weather forecasters on the evening news, had expected snow. After all, it's April, Spring already, and the daffodils, tulips and snowdrops are already popping their heads out of the cold earth, seeking fresh air and a little gentle sunshine. I love it when those flowers appear, don't you? Really makes you feel like summer's on the way."

Andy knew that it was unusual to get snow in Spring, especially here in Eastbourne on the South Coast of England, a place generally known for its mild climate. A place where people dreamt of retiring to, once they had finished their working life. For this, his first police posting after training college, he had relocated from Northumberland, close to the Scottish border. The weather was much harsher up there and he was already enjoying the milder temperatures of the South Coast.

"MY MUM and Dad moved here 10 years ago and are loving it: they enjoy being able to stroll down to the beach to meet their new friends for lunch in one of the little seaside cafes, or go for adventures to nearby Beachy Head or the Seven Sisters. They say they wish they'd done it years ago. They can do whatever takes their fancy. So much nicer than having to get up with the alarm clock every day and trudge to boring old office jobs as they had to for the last 40 years. Now they're free agents."

. . .

SADLY, Betty and her husband Ian *weren't* free agents. *They* were trying desperately to save enough money to put down as a deposit on a property of their own, but having spent the first two years of their married life paying rent on a tiny little flat in a rather grotty part of town, they had realised they were getting nowhere fast. So, when Betty's parents had suggested they move in with them for a year or two, rent free, it had made a lot of sense. The only problem was that they both did shift work (because it paid much better than ordinary jobs) so it meant that they were often like ships passing in the night, unable to spend much quality time together.

Having explained all that, she continued.

"So, this morning, like every other morning, I had to leave the house by 5.45 to make sure I got to work on time. My job, working in the offices of the local D.I.Y superstore, doesn't start till 6.30, but I always like to allow plenty of time in case my old car doesn't start".

"I WALKED SLOWLY down the garden path, trying not slip. The crisp white snow looked beautiful, but I knew from bitter experience that once it turned to ice it could be lethal. I've still got a few scars on my leg from where I slipped and fell on black ice ten years ago."

BETTY and her family lived on a street full of old Victorian houses, sturdy brick homes that had originally been built back in the late 1800's for working class families. They were exactly like the houses you could find on any street, in any town or city, in England. Plain red brick terraced houses, with tiny front gardens and long narrow plots behind. They had been built in the days of horse and carriages rather than motor cars, so there were no garages attached. Instead, there was a narrow alleyway that ran behind the houses, just a rough track really, but wide enough to accommodate a car, so some homeowners had built freestanding garages at the bottom of their gardens with gates that opened onto the lane.

Of course this was the 1980's, so lots of people owned cars now. Why, some families, like Betty's, had several. These garages were too small to accommodate more than one vehicle, so Betty and her husband always had to park theirs outside in the lane.

"We've only got small old cars, that's all we can afford right now and we always try to make sure they're tucked tightly against the fence, so they won't block anyone's access, but of course there's always a few grumpy people who like to moan."

She paused. She knew you shouldn't speak ill of the dead.

"That Mr. Jones for example. His wife was lovely, but he was a miserable old bloke. Well spoken, well dressed, but lacking in much charm in my view. He might be a bank manager, stuck up and full of his own importance, but I don't think he was a very pleasant man at all. Not my idea of a gentleman, nothing like my perfect husband Ian, or my lovely kind dad."

"Oh Betty love, don't say that. The poor man is dead."

"I know Mum. But just because he's lying out there in the snow doesn't mean he's suddenly a nice person."

The young policeman smiled to himself. This spirited

young woman was just his cup of tea, what a shame she was married.

He smiled at her, encouraging her to continue talking.

"I ALWAYS TRIED to avoid him as much as possible, he gave me the creeps a bit.

If I was ever in the lane when he roared up in his shiny new car I'd rush indoors so I didn't have to make conversation with him. His car was as flashy as he was, quite unsuitable for a middle-aged man in my opinion. My mum always said that his claret coloured Jaguar XJ6, with its fast engine and leather interior, was the sign of an "old bloke trying to regain his lost youth."

Her mum, sitting at the other side of the kitchen table shook her head. That girl of hers was too outspoken for her own good sometimes.

"ANYWAY, this snowy morning, his posh car was all tucked up in the garage at the back of number 47. I expect he would have taken a taxi to work that morning, rather than risk his precious car getting damaged by more falling snow, or by all the salt they chuck on the main roads to stop ice forming. He was very precious about that car, my mum often said that he treated that car better than he did his own wife!"

She seemed to have calmed down a bit and was now in her stride, quite enjoying telling her dramatic story.

"IT WAS VERY dark in the lane that morning. There are only two streetlights, one at the top of the alley and one at the bottom. This meant that the bit in between, my bit, was rather gloomy. It

wouldn't be daylight for another hour or so, but I'm used to leaving home in the dark. I always carry my big torch with me. Luckily my car was parked right outside the back gate and as I put my key into the lock I looked around, making sure there was nothing to bump into as I reversed into the lane."

She paused for dramatic effect.

"I noticed a big lump in the snow: obviously someone had put their rubbish bags out overnight and the falling snow had covered it. I hate it when people do that, put it out the night before so they don't have to get up early on bin day. It attracts all sorts: cats, dogs, seagulls and vermin and sometimes they rip open the bags and then the lane is full of peoples unwanted food scraps.

Anyway, I was in a hurry as usual, but didn't want to risk running over the bags and make a big mess, she I got out and walked over to the pile."

"I TRIED *to kick the bags out of the way, then I realised it was a body. A dead body. And then I screamed."*

She burst into tears and her mum spoke instead.

"This is a really quiet street usually. A very respectable place. But everyone heard her screaming. My poor girl. Her screams echoed around the dark lane. Lights went on in all the houses and after a few minutes people emerged, mostly in their nightclothes. Apparently my Betty carried on screaming until I appeared and took her inside. She was in a right state. First time she's ever seen a dead body."

IT TOOK a while for the police officers to get a response to their knocking. Vera Jones had been fast asleep, quite unaware of the drama unfolding in the lane.

.   .   .

WHEN THEY TOLD her of her husband's demise, It had been such a shock for her. She looked as though she might faint, so young Andy made her a cup of tea, while the female officer gently led her to an armchair.

"WE ARE SO sorry Mrs Jones. Is there anyone we can call to come and stay with you. You shouldn't be alone after such a shock."

"OH THANK YOU DEAR. No, I'll be fine on my own. But perhaps you could let my neighbours know. Number 73, Martha. Just in case I need any shopping or anything. I'm sorry if there's not much milk left for your cups of tea. I was going to pop out and get some more first thing in the morning, before Herbert got up. He does like a nice cup of milky coffee with his toast and marmalade."

With that she burst into tears, realising that her husband was never again going to demand a milky coffee with two spoonful's of sugar.

They let her calm down for a few minutes before continuing.

"MRS JONES, did your husband have heart problems or anything that might make him collapse? I am sorry to ask, please don't answer if it upsets you, we can always pop back later on, once you're over the worst of the shock."

It seemed to the young policeman that Vera Jones had aged ten years in the last ten minutes. She was obviously in deep shock, as anyone would be, having heard that their husband had dropped dead. And the shock of learning that he had frozen to death, lying outside for hours, right outside his own home, while she had presumably been tucked up in a warm bed fast asleep.

"I'm sorry to ask this, but did you not notice that your husband didn't come home last night?" He blushed as he spoke, it seemed such an intrusive question to ask, especially of someone old enough to be his mother.

"Oh my dear, Herbert was often out late, at various meetings or the pub. When I was younger I used to stay up and wait for him to come home, making sure I was there if he fancied a cup of tea or a bit of toast, but in the last few years he insisted I just went to bed when I felt like it. Said I wasn't getting any younger and needed my beauty sleep. And of course I have to get up early to get to work in time. I work at Bobby's, the department store."

SHE ANSWERED ALL THEIR QUESTIONS, even though at times she was close to tears.

They all hated seeing her in such distress. It was the worst part of their jobs as police officers, having to deliver such devastating news.

"WELL THANK you so much Mrs. Jones. My deepest sympathy for your loss. I am sorry to say that there will have to be an inquest, even though there doesn't appear to be any suspicious circum-stances. Even in tragic accidents like this, we have to make sure that no stone is left unturned. We will be in touch once the coroner has released the body. Please don't hesitate to contact us if you have any questions or think of anything else we should know."

2

AFTERWARDS

Like all dramas, the excitement passed quickly and after a few days everyone just got back on with their lives. The neighbours were questioned of course, the police had to do their job after all, even if it appeared to be an open and shut case. Betty had to attend the inquest to give evidence. She was still a bit shaken up and so had been given two weeks compassionate leave from her job. After all it wasn't every day you discovered a dead body right outside your house.

THE INQUEST WAS HELD. The police gave their evidence and witness statements were read. The grieving widow, looking pale and dignified, sat quietly, listening intently to every word.

"Herbert Henry Jones. Age 57. Bank Manager. Married, no children."

"Frozen to death."

"Misadventure."

"Accidental death, although there was excess alcohol in the body."

"No evidence of illegal drugs."

"Injuries consistent with slipping, falling and banging head on rough concrete path."

"Some slight bruising to front of body, cause unknown."

"Mr. Jones was known to have minor heart problems, but it is doubtful this contributed to his death."

"A sad accident. No indication of foul play."

Verdict: Death by misadventure.

Case closed.

VERA ELIZABETH JONES had never expected to be widowed so young. She had always imagined that her husband Herbert would outlive her. He had always seemed so full of life, so vibrant, so passionate.

They had met when she was just nineteen years old, a naïve and impressionable young woman and he had swept her off her feet with his charm, his brooding good looks and his patter. He was only a bank clerk then, but he had big ambitions and was determined to become a bank manager.

"You watch, my girl, one day I'll be one of the most important men in this town. Someone that people will look up to."

SHE HAD BEEN VERY IMPRESSED. He was exactly the sort of man she had always hoped to marry. A man who would love her forever and provide well for her and her children.

She had met him at the local nightclub. He and a group of his mates were from the next town, some 10 miles away, and they had decided to go to Eastbourne that night looking for "*fresh talent.*" It was the 1960's, the Swinging Sixties some called it, and to many young men of that era it was still quite acceptable to treat women as playthings: to wolf whistle and fondle their bodies as you danced.

But Herbert wasn't like that. He acted like a true gentleman, always kind, always courteous: opening doors and walking on the kerbside of the pavement (an old English custom he had explained to Vera, that was intended to ensure that delicate ladies never got splashed by passing cars, or toppled off the kerb.) She had been impressed with his rather old fashioned manners, it made such a change from having to fight off other boys she dated who felt entitled to explore her body with their big rough hands.

THEY WERE MARRIED A YEAR LATER. In many ways she hardly knew him, they had only spent three evenings a week together and barely any weekends. He had explained that he was frightfully busy studying, he was so determined to rise through the ranks, to become a bank manager and sit in a wood panelled office all day, issuing instructions to his minions.

She didn't much like the way he spoke about other people, people he considered lesser than himself, and there were one or two other aspects of his character that worried her a little, but she put all those fears aside, put on her beautiful long white dress and smiled for all the wedding photos.

AT FIRST IT had been lovely, she had been so busy trying to be the ideal wife that she hardly noticed his bad points. If he was grumpy, she just put it down to him being tired, what with working in the bank all day and then studying every night and all weekend. She knew how much his career meant to him, so she tried to be as supportive as possible. Of course it meant that *she* was always rather tired too: as well as running the home and attending to her husband's every need, she had a full time job working in the local department store. She had been there since she left school and had worked her way up to being in charge of a whole department: ladies scarves and gloves. There was very little she didn't know about such things. She could talk for ages about the very best and softest leather gloves, or the finest patterned silk scarves. She knew the best suppliers and the best factories and one day she secretly hoped to be invited to go on a buying trip to Milan in Italy, with her boss Miss Hardcastle, and Mr. Tripp the store owner. It was a well-known secret that those two had been lovers for more than 20 years and would probably have married had it not been for the fact that Mr. Tripp had been married to the formidable Mrs. Tripp for the last 25 years and she was most reluctant to get a divorce, as she would then lose her enviable lifestyle. Being the wife of the largest department store owner in the town brought many benefits and so much prestige, and despite being unfulfilled in her marriage and only too aware that her husbands heart lay elsewhere, she was determined to cling on until the bitter end. As for Mr. Tripp, it was rather good for his ego to have two women fighting for his attention. He enjoyed having a wife at home and a younger, prettier mistress at his workplace.

3

THE FUNERAL

The funeral was very well attended. The old stone church was almost overflowing with mourners. It seemed that many people wanted to pay their respects to Herbert, or perhaps they were just curious, after all it wasn't every day that your local bank manager froze to death outside his own home.

Vera, the widow, sat quietly in the front row, flanked on either side by two young men: Henry and Hugh, nephews of her late husband. Having not been fortunate enough to have children of her own, these boys had been an important part of her life for many years and she was grateful for their support today.

"*Welcome to you all. We are here today to celebrate the life of a much loved husband, uncle, brother and friend to many.*

Herbert Henry Jones was a pillar of this society, a respected bank manager and a man who did much good for his community..."

. . .

VERA SQUIRMED IN HER SEAT. How she hated hearing him spoken about like this. She had always been so private, keeping her feelings to herself and now she was expected to share all her emotions and memories with everyone in this church. Before the coffin was carried in, she had glanced around and noticed lots of familiar faces: several of their neighbours of course, including young Betty who had found the body. Betty was there with her mum, both of them were looking pale and upset, dressed in their best black clothes. Vera looked down at her own outfit: a rather nice well cut black dress and matching jacket in a fine wool mix. It had been a little expensive, but she had bought it at the department store with her staff discount. The discount was so good that she had also treated herself to a little pillbox hat with a black net veil attached. She had known it would be useful to hide her tears.

Several of her friends from the shop were sitting in the rows behind: Mr. and Mrs. Tripp, Miss Hardcastle and Jennifer and Lucy from the Ladieswear department.

Two whole pews were filled with Herberts colleagues from the bank. She knew that he would have hated hearing them referred to as his "colleagues." To him they were just his employees, the people he directed to keep the business of the bank running smoothly. Still, it seemed he must have been a good boss, as there were so many of those people, both past and present staff, attending his funeral today.

THERE WERE ALSO QUITE a few people that Vera didn't recognise, but that wasn't altogether surprising, as she rarely left the house apart from going to work every day. Herbert had always preferred to keep his home and work life quite separate.

"Oh come on old girl, you'd be bored stiff having to make small talk with all my cronies. None of the other wives will be there."

"Come on now Vera, do you really want to hang about all evening sipping on your one glass of that horrible sweet white wine?

I'm going to be too busy making new contacts and doing deals, to be able to babysit you. You'd be much better off staying at home and watching your favourite soap opera on the telly."

SHE HAD ALWAYS RATHER RESENTED BEING RELEGATED to being *"the little woman indoors"* but over the years she had become accustomed to being left at home while he went to dinners, functions and even business weekends away without her. She knew she had lost her sparkle a bit. It was hard to shine when your husband, the one man who was supposed to find you desirable, obviously preferred the company of other people. Still, at least he had never been unfaithful or abandoned her. They still lived in the house they had bought from her parents when they were first married: a solid three bedroomed brick house, built in the late Victorian era. A terraced house in a street of similar houses. With a long alleyway running behind.

The alleyway where Herbert, her husband of more than 35 years, had died. Frozen to death. She shuddered and felt the tears rolling down her cheeks. At least the veil hid them. She had always been a very private person and saw no need to share her emotions now.

· · ·

"My Uncle Herbert was a fine man, a real gentleman. He taught me and my brother Hugh so much. Our dad died when we were young you see, so Uncle Herb and Aunty Vera were the only family us and our mum had really. Our mum Joan really loved her brother and I'm just glad she's not still alive to see how horribly he died. It would have broken her heart. Thanks for everything Herbert, we'll really miss you."

"I knew Herbert for 46 years. We started at the Grammar school together when we were just eleven and we stayed friends all these years. Of course there was always a bit of rivalry, Herbert being a banker and me working at an insurance company, but despite that we stayed good mates all these years. We even went on a few business trips together, leaving our wives at home!"

THE NEXT SPEAKER WAS A WOMAN, probably in her late 50's, although with her dyed blonde hair and heavy make-up she could have been older.

"I've known Herbert for more than 30 years, ever since he first set foot in my pub. I run the Leg Of Mutton public house opposite his bank building, so every day, rain or shine, he's popped over for a couple of pints and a bit of lunch. I'm going to miss his smiling face and those bow ties."

THERE WAS A BIT OF LAUGHTER. Everyone knew about Herberts penchant for bow ties. He had worn them every day, they had become his trademark.

. . .

A FEW MORE PEOPLE SPOKE, singing his praises and reminiscing about their memories of the deceased man. And then it was over. The final hymn was sung, the departing prayers spoken and the velvet curtain closed, taking the mortal remains of Herbert Henry Jones to the fire and his eternal resting place.

OUTSIDE THE CHURCH everyone crowded around Vera, wanting to express their sympathy to the grieving widow. After what seemed to her like an eternity, a continuous stream of *"so sorry for your loss, he was a good man,"* she finally found herself back in her own home. Her two nephews had left and gone back to their own lives and their own families and it would probably be some time before she saw them again. She had no doubt that they cared, they had been such sweet little boys and had become fine young men, but now they were both married and living some distance away. And everyone knows the expression *"A son is a son till he gets him a wife."* Still, they would almost certainly turn up for the will reading next week, so at least she'd see them again then.

Alone in the house she had shared with Herbert for so long, Vera sat lost in thought. She thought about all the times they had shared, all the years of companionship, the occasional arguments about money. She remembered how she had resented him for buying his flashy brand new Jaguar car, just weeks after he had explained that all they could afford for *her* was an old second-hand Ford Escort. She had been really cross at the time, especially as *all* her wages went into their joint account, but as usual she had acquiesced to keep the peace. He had explained that it was extremely important that the local bank manager was seen to be driving a top of the range car, apparently he needed to look very successful, both for his own standing and that of the institution.

There had been so many times over the years that she had given in, neglecting her own hopes and dreams in order to keep the peace and make him happy. She regretted that a bit now, now that she was alone. Alone to cope with the house, the finances and everything that entailed. Mind you, her nephews Henry and Hugh had promised to help as much as they could. Of course, they both expected to receive sizeable bequests from their uncles estate, so they were bound to be helpful! They had even offered to take Herberts Jaguar car off her hands, but for now it comforted her to see it sitting in the garage, a small reminder of her husband. Maybe later on she would feel like getting rid of it, it was far too big and powerful for her to drive. For now she was content with her old Ford Escort, but maybe, once the will was sorted out, she would indulge and buy herself a newer model.

SHE THOUGHT TOO ABOUT ALL the people who had been at the funeral. She had been surprised to see so many, she hadn't realised just how popular and well-liked her husband had been. All those lovely speeches people had made about him. It had come as a bit of a surprise. But then of course, she had known him as a husband, not just as *"a perfect gentleman."*

.   .   .

LOTS of her neighbours had attended the funeral. Having lived in the street for so many years, she knew them all by sight and had been touched that they had bothered to turn up. Of course she realised that some of it was mere curiosity, after all it wasn't every day a dead body turned up in their street. And of course it had been advertised in the local newspaper, both on the front page news *"Local Bank Manager Discovered Frozen To Death"* and in the obituary column on the back page. The black and white picture alongside the article was one a local photographer had taken a couple of years earlier when Herbert was voted Businessman Of the Year. He had been very proud of that and insisted on having a copy of the photo enlarged and put in a flashy gold frame. It stood in pride of place, alongside the trophy, on his office desk in the spare bedroom. A room that Vera only ventured into twice a week, to flick a feather duster over the book-shelves and ornaments and to run the vacuum cleaner across the carpet. Herbert had always been very insistent that she didn't linger in there. *"I have very important papers on my desk, please make sure you never move or interfere with them in any way. And never touch my computer, they are delicate things. I am one of the first people in this town to own a personal computer you know."*

Vera didn't doubt that. Herbert was very fond of treating himself to all the latest gadgets and as soon as he heard about the new Amstrad home computer he had been deter-mined to own one. Luckily one of his bank customers had a shop that stocked all the latest models, so he had been able to buy one at a much reduced price. She had been a bit cross, after all he did all his work in his office at the bank, so she didn't really understand why he needed such a thing at home. And of course, once the next model was introduced, he would probably want to upgrade, much like he did with his cars. Apparently these home computers were becoming all the rage now and he had explained to her that by the turn of the century, the year 2000, there would be numerous different models available. She barely listened as he droned on about P.C's, floppy disks, Sony and IBM. All she really wanted was some new curtains for the sitting room, but he had told her in no uncertain terms that there was nothing wrong with the brown velvet ones her mum had installed more than 30 years earlier.

VERY FEW OF their neighbours had ever set foot in Herbert and Vera's house and that made her all the more grateful that they had bothered to turn up at his funeral. In the old days, when her mum and dad had lived in the house, it had always been full of people, they had loved entertaining and throwing parties. But Herbert was not keen on visitors, he said that he spent all his days talking to people, so when he got home he just wanted to put his feet up and have some peace and quiet.

VERA HAD TRIED to chat to people at the morning tea following the funeral service. Most people were kind and friendly, but a few others, mostly women she didn't recognise, were a little aloof. She guessed they must be his customers from the bank. There was so much about his working life that she didn't know.

4

AFTER THE FUNERAL

As anyone who has lost somebody knows, the period after the funeral, after all the mourners have left, is often the worst time. Suddenly, particularly if you have been widowed, you are all alone, often for the first time in many years and it can be a very lonely and miserable time.

Vera knew she was lucky. She had some really good neighbours, people who she knew would pop in and check on her from time to time and she had her workmates, women she had known since she first started at the shop when she was sixteen. So many years ago. Sometimes she found it hard to believe where all those years had gone. Whilst her colleagues had filled those years with babies, teenagers and now grandchildren, she had only had Herbert to take care of. In the school holidays she had also had his nephews, but once they got to be teenagers they had been less interested in bucket and spade seaside holidays with Uncle Herb and Aunty Vera, so she hadn't seen so much of them in recent years. But she felt sure she could call on them in a crisis.

Although sadly she realised that they would probably visit her less often now. At the will reading she knew they had been rather disappointed not to receive more from Herbert's estate. They had obviously been expecting a windfall rather than a dribble, and although she thought that the amounts of 10,000 pounds each were generous, they were obviously disappointed and had expected more. That evening, in an attempt to cheer them up, she had suggested that they might like to sell Herberts Jaguar and split the proceeds between the two of them, thus bumping up their inheritance a little.. They had agreed instantly and driven the car away that very evening, obviously keen to put it on the market and recoup some extra cash as quickly as possible.

After they had gone, Vera stood in the empty garage and shed a few tears. Herberts pride and joy, his Jaguar, was now gone from her life forever, just like her dear deceased husband.

5

TED (CAR DEALER)

A few weeks later, in an attempt to cheer herself up, she popped to the Ford dealer in town and traded in her old car for a shiny new one in a very fetching colour. *Wild Strawberry Metallic* they called it. It was rather thrilling as she had never owned a new car before. In the past she had just had to be content with old second hand ones. She just hoped that the neighbours wouldn't disapprove and think she was being rather selfish, playing the merry widow while her husband's body was hardly cold.

Ted, the owner of the Ford dealership, was delighted to see her spoiling herself. He had known Vera since they were children, in fact he had been in love with her since he was 15. She had been the prettiest girl in Eastbourne he reckoned. But years of living with that rather controlling husband had definitely dimmed down her sparkle a bit. That made Ted sad and rather angry. Not only had Herbert Jones stolen his first love, but in his opinion, he hadn't treated her very well either. A girl like Vera should be treated like a queen and he knew that Herbert hadn't done that. It had bugged him for years and had often been a bone of contention.

"Oh come on love, you don't know what goes on behind closed doors. Maybe he treats her better at home than he does in public."

Ted had sighed as his wife of 25 years continued speaking.

"Just because you loved her first and probably do still love her a bit, doesn't mean her husband is a brute. I've never seen a mark on her and she's always nicely dressed. He obviously doesn't try and control her spending."

Ted winced. He knew she was still angry with him for not wanting to go on that trip to Spain. He just considered it a waste of money, spending hundreds of pounds to sit on a crowded beach, when they had a perfectly nice beach here at home. Of course Eastbourne beach was a bit pebbly, not covered in fine sand like the ones he'd seen in the glossy travel brochures she'd stuck under his nose.

"Oh love, don't be cross. I promise we'll have a nice holiday, I just don't fancy Spain that's all. What about a nice week in the Lake District in a caravan?"

He knew that Vera loved travelling too. Although she didn't just want a cheap package trip to Spain like his wife did. She wanted a lot more than that. Every time he fixed her car he found travel brochures on the front seat. He had asked her about them once.

"Oh Ted, I've always wanted to travel, since I was a little girl. I'd love to see the world, but Herbert won't go anywhere, certainly not abroad. We went to Scotland once. I loved it, all the mountains and the lakes, but he hated it, said there were too many midges and castles. He much prefers a week in Torquay. I just pick up

these travel brochures when I'm feeling fed up. It cheers me up a bit you see, imagining all the places I could go."

TED KNEW that he was being a bit unfair to his wife. She had been a good wife to him all these years and a wonderful mother to their three children. She had also carried the burden of knowing that he was still a little in love with Vera, the one who got away, the first girl he had ever loved. She had coped patiently with his slightly adolescent behaviour: the way he always gazed longingly at Vera whenever he saw her all dressed up at a public function. The way his heart fluttered whenever she popped into his car dealership, asking for advice about a problem with her car. Of course that had rarely happened, certainly not as often as he would have liked. Herbert kept a tight grip on her, so she was rarely seen in public without him. But Ted knew she worked at the department store, so he sometimes popped in there hoping to see her.

The other reason Ted didn't like Herbert Jones much was because he was something of a skinflint, not just with his wife Vera, but with everyone he did business with. He always expected a hefty discount wherever he shopped or dined and was well known for expressing the opinion that any establishment was lucky to have his custom, *"After all as the local bank manager I have a certain standing in the community. It would be in your best interests to give me a nice little discount."*

ALTHOUGH HE ATTENDED the funeral out of respect for Vera, Ted was not in the least upset that Herbert Jones had frozen to death.

6

PAUL AND DAVE KING

Paul and Dave King were twin brothers and would probably have been best friends even if they weren't related. They were so alike: they liked the same food, the same books, the same cars and the same women. They had only been 23 years old when their father decided to retire, leaving his car dealership to them. They had been working there since they left school, so he had known it would be in good hands when he and their stepmother decided to spend six months of every year in Spain. Nowadays, even after them being in charge for more than 20 years, he still rang the garage daily, just to check up on things. In reality he knew they were more than capable of making a huge success of the business he had started, in fact they were making more money now than he could have imagined in his wildest dreams, but he enjoyed still feeling involved. They loved their father dearly and always looked forward to his calls and visits.

Paul ran the sales side and Dave was in charge of the workshop and all the mechanics. They both worked hard, they knew how lucky they were to have inherited a ready-made business, one that they could improve and put their own stamp on and they never took it for granted. It had given them both a very good lifestyle. Good enough to each own large houses with a bit of land, father several children and have a few wives between them. Now that they had matured, their biggest dream was to meet a woman they could devote themselves to for the rest of their lives, without having any desire to stray as they had done so often in the past.

So far neither of them had been very successful in that respect. They had both married lovely women, women that most men would have been content to spend the rest of their lives with, but Paul and Dave had both had one too many extramarital affairs, culminating in expensive divorces. Currently they were both casually dating young Russian women, beautiful twenty something year olds: good eye candy, but in their hearts they knew that those attractive and attentive girls were really only interested in their expensive lifestyles, fast cars and open wallets.

The problem was that Paul and Dave King were both incredibly good-looking. They had worked their way through most of the female population of the town over the years. Even now, in their early fifties, they still turned heads: these two six feet tall, dark haired (although greying slightly at the temples these days) charming men who whizzed around town in their top of the range Jaguar cars. Of course they could afford the latest models as they owned the dealership.

.   .   .

Herbert Henry Jones had been one of their regular customers. Although he had spent a good deal of money in their establishment over the years, he was not one of their favourite clients. In fact they both rather despised him. Quite apart from the fact that he always insisted on an hefty discount, implying that *his* position as the local bank manager entitled him to special treatment, he refused to advertise their business in any way. Most people they gave big discounts to understood that it was a *"you scratch my back and I'll scratch yours"* kind of arrangement, but they knew that Herbert, as soon as he pulled off their forecourt in his brand new shiny Jaguar (he always ordered the latest model with every possible extra) would stop down the road and remove the sticky back windscreen sign advertising *"Kings Motors, the best in Sussex for all your Jaguar needs."*

Apart from his meanness, they disliked him for other reasons. Of course they bumped into him often, at Rotary Club meetings, local Business Association meetings and occasionally at parties or Masonic Balls. Herbert wasn't a Mason, but they both were and they had heard from their peers that he was desperate to be invited to join the secret organisation. However, it seemed that despite his standing as a respected local bank manager, there were not many people willing to stand up and recommend his membership. But in return for the odd overdraft or loan facility, other members sometimes invited him to their balls, which were quite grand affairs held at smart hotels or function rooms. The twins met his wife Vera at some of these events and had remarked afterwards that it was a shame that such a fine looking, friendly and intelligent woman was stuck with an arrogant self-opinionated man like Herbert.

They had also heard, through the club grapevine, that he

was a known womaniser and didn't treat anyone very well. In fact some of the stories were pretty awful. They tried to take them with a pinch of salt, no scandals had ever appeared in the local newspaper, but they were well connected to all sorts of people in the town, so they heard most things.

They were always particularly disgusted to hear of someones business failing because they had been unable to get an extended overdraft or loan from the bank. As local businessmen themselves, they understood how hard it was to keep a business afloat, particularly during difficult economic times. Surely that was what a local bank manager was for, to assist local businesses in their time of need. Paul and Dave knew of several decent men who had lost their livelihood because the bank foreclosed on their loans. Unfairly in most cases, as if they had just been allowed a little leeway, a few more months trading would have seen them getting out of the red and making a profit.

UNFORTUNATELY PAUL KING WAS A GAMBLER. He had managed to keep it hidden from everyone for years. Not even his brother Dave was aware of the extent of his addiction. He knew of course that Paul liked a little flutter. They had both enjoyed the excitement of going to the casinos on their trip to Las Vegas and they always bet on horse races, but Dave had no idea that Paul had been secretly going to illegal card games, run by rather disreputable types, who had no qualms about watching him lose all his money, night after night.

The problem got worse once he got tangled up with his Russian girlfriend. It was always rather a thrill to walk into the card games with a beautiful young woman on his arm. A beautiful very young woman, with long curly hair and bright red fingernails, who wore low cut, very short tight dresses that enhanced her voluptuous figure. A woman that most men would fantasise about.

Unfortunately, the particular young woman that Paul had been involved with for more than a year now, had very expensive tastes. She would only shop in designer stores, go to the most fashionable bars and restaurants and expected long weekends away in swanky hotels. His money was running out fast and the only way to keep up with her demands was to gamble. Sadly, he frequently lost and in the end, after a fortnight of frittering away several tens of thousands of pounds, he was forced to visit the bank and ask for a temporary overdraft.

"Now my dear chap. I'm at a bit of a loss to understand why you're suddenly so hard up. When I see you at the Business Association meetings, you're always saying how well your car dealerships doing."

"Oh this is nothing to do with the business. It's a personal overdraft I'm seeking. Nothing to do with my brother or the business."

"So, I gather you want to keep it secret? Our little secret? Perhaps in return, if I grant you this overdraft, you could see your way to nominating me for membership of your Masonic Lodge?"

Paul had no choice. The man had him over a barrel. It was obvious that the bank manager had no scruples: if he refused to do what the wretched man asked, he wouldn't put it past him to tell his brother Dave about his gambling.

· · ·

In the end he told his brother anyway. The guilt of keeping such a big secret rested heavily on his shoulders. He knew that the Russian girlfriend would probably not be in his life forever, but his brother Dave hopefully would be.

"Don't you worry Paul. We'll get through this somehow. And I'm damned if we're going to let that monstrous man become a Mason. Over my dead body."

No, Herbert Henry Jones was not a good man in the opinion of the King brothers. There was not a shred of decency in him as far as they were concerned. So although they attended his funeral, neither Paul nor Dave King were in the least sorry to hear that he had died.

7

POLLY EVANS

Polly Evans was 45 years old and ran a bookshop in the Old Town area of Eastbourne. She had inherited it from her parents and could never imagine doing anything else.

She had been born in the little flat upstairs and from a very young age had helped her parents in the business. It was in her blood she reckoned, she loved books, any kind of books. Old ones, new ones, second-hand or pristine, it really didn't make any difference to her, she just loved everything about them: the feel of holding them in her hands, the smell of new ink or the rather musty smell of the old books. She loved the contents, all the stuff she learnt from reading them and the emotions they stirred.

By the time she was 20 years old she was practically running the place. Her mum and dad knew their business was safe in her capable hands, so they often took off for weekend jaunts or even short trips to Europe, ostensibly to look for new stock, but in reality they just wanted to spend some quality time together: they were still madly in love, even after 21 years of marriage. Polly was their only and much loved child and their example had taught her everything she knew about love.

IT WAS a sunny Spring day when she first laid eyes on Herbert Jones. The good looking young man had come into the shop looking for car maintenance books.

"Oh, I'm so sorry. We don't keep anything like that. Not much call for them you see. Have you tried the library?"

Any red blooded man would have been entranced by the young woman. Polly was tall, nearly six feet in height, with a slim yet curvaceous body, long red curly hair and big brown eyes. That day she was wearing tight fitting blue jeans and a red silk shirt that showed off her youthful curves.

He came into the shop every day for the next week, always asking about something he knew she probably didn't stock. Her parents were away, they had popped over to Paris for a romantic jaunt, so Polly was alone in the shop.

After five visits she weakened and accepted his offer of dinner at the local pub, The Leg of Mutton. She could walk there and knew most of the pub regulars, so even if the date didn't go well, she knew she would be safe. To her surprise, she rather enjoyed the evening, and ended up seeing him every day for the following fortnight.

Unfortunately he was very persuasive. He used all his charm to woo her and because she had grown up surrounded by love and knew nothing else, she believed him when he said he was madly in love with her and wanted them to get married as soon as possible. She had read enough romance novels to know that tall dark handsome men like him were few and far between, so should be snapped up as soon as possible.

Of course the inevitable happened. He had his wicked way with her and had already moved on to his next conquest by the time she realised she was pregnant. Sad and ashamed, she refused to reveal the name of her baby's father, but of course her lovely parents scooped her up and protected her, sheltering her from too much of the gossip flying around the town.

Now, years later, it was just her and her daughter Vanessa running the place. Although her mum and dad were still alive, they had moved into a little flat by the seafront and only occasionally popped into the shop to help.

The scandal of Vanessa's birth was long forgotten, her lovely girl, now a beautiful young woman in her early twenties, was a replica of her mother Polly, with her long curly red hair and big brown eyes. The local boys were always trying to chat her up, but Vanessa was having none of it, there was no way she intended to make the same mistake her mum had.

HERBERT HENRY JONES, now a respectable bank manager, never knew that he had fathered a daughter.

But Polly would never forget how casually he had treated her, casting her aside as soon as another desirable young woman came along. At the time of their liaison she had not realised that he was married, he had kept that little secret to himself. She would never have given up her virginity to him if she had realised he had no intention of marrying her.

She had never told anyone who Vanessa's father was, but because they worked in the same town, she saw him often, strutting around in his grey pin striped suits and flashy red bow ties, acting as if he owned the place. Occasionally he would glance in her direction, noticing that she was still a beautiful woman, but he realised, from the withering looks she sent in his direction, that there was no way he should approach her, she was definitely now off limits.

It was just as well that Polly could not read his thoughts.

"Shame, as I vaguely remember that she had been one of my more successful conquests, but of course that was years ago now. Mind you, if I was a younger man I might try my hand at that daughter of hers, she is a pretty little thing, just like her mother used to be."

Although Polly had never told anyone who had fathered her child, people talked. Luckily it didn't seem to occur to any of them that the bank manager might be to blame. After all, he was a respected pillar of the community and had a lovely wife. A good looking charming woman, who still kept herself looking good. Polly felt really sorry for her, Vera was a lovely woman, kind and generous. They often had a chat when the older woman popped into the bookshop. She was a big fan of all the old romantic novels: the Jane Austens and Charlotte Brontes. Lately she had taken to reading works by more modern authors, but they were always of the same genre: tales of love, marriage and happily ever after. Polly often wondered if she was dreaming of a life different to the one she had with Herbert, the dull and rather boring bank manager. Of course, twenty years ago, he had been slim, had long hair and sideburns and was rather handsome. In those days, when he wasn't at work, he had worn a leather jacket and ridden a Harley Davison. Then, he could easily have wooed any woman he wanted. Now he was rather bald and a little stocky, with thick bushy eyebrows and a moustache, and his face had that rosy tinge associated with too much drinking. Women didn't fall at his feet as they used to, but he used his position as the local bank manager to get people to do what he wanted.

Every time she caught sight of him in the street she shuddered. He may be a respectable gentleman and a pillar of society now, but she knew, from bitter experience, that underneath the expensive grey pin stripe suits and flashy red bow ties, he was rotten to the core.

She really hoped that one day he would suffer in the same way he had made so many other people suffer.

Polly was not sorry to hear that he had died. She, along with most of the other shopkeepers in the town, attended his funeral, but she certainly did not shed any tears for him.

8

———

BETTY

Betty still wasn't sleeping very well. It was good that she was still on extended sick leave as since that awful morning she hated closing her eyes. Every time she did she was standing in the lane, looking at his frozen body lying there, covered in snow. It had been such a dreadful shock. Somehow she had got through the inquest and the funeral, but she still could not get that awful sight out of her mind.

Still, she knew it was much worse for Vera, his wife. She had lost her husband. Betty knew how heartbroken she would be if anything happened to her Ian. Of course they'd only been married a couple of years, nowhere near as long as Herbert and Vera, so she guessed the widow must be utterly distraught.

"MUM, I think I'm going to pop round and see Mrs. Jones. She must be feeling a bit sad and lonely. I've got nothing else to do till I go back to work next week, so I might as well see if I can cheer her

up. I'll pop to the shops and buy her some cakes and a bunch of flowers, do you think that'll be ok?"

Betty's mum smiled to herself. What a lovely kind girl her daughter had turned out to be. Always thinking of other people.

"That's a great idea love. Perhaps get some nice daffs or tulips, nothing that looks like funeral flowers. She'll appreciate you visiting I'm sure."

BETTY HAD NEVER BEEN inside the Jones house before and she was surprised how old fashioned it was. Mrs. Jones (Vera) had always seemed quite modern and well dressed, but her house was totally different to what Betty had imagined. She had expected to see lovely modern furniture and bright curtains and cushions. Instead there was a sea of dark brown heavy old fashioned wooden cabinets and tables, brown and cream swirly patterned carpets and brown velvet curtains. Even the paintings on the wall seemed to be brown: gloomy scenes of autumn, or dark seascapes. The only bright thing in the room was Vera herself. She was wearing a knitted twinset in a pretty shade of pink with a pleated skirt in a matching shade. On her feet were pink slippers edged in fur. Even her lipstick and glasses were pink. She seemed delighted to see Betty.

"Oh my dear it is so kind of you to visit me. Would you like a cup of tea?"

Betty followed her into the kitchen and was relieved to see it wasn't as gloomy as the sitting room. Instead the cupboards were painted cream and the floor was covered in a yellow patterned vinyl. There was a display of bright yellow mugs on one shelf and a pile of well-thumbed cookery books on another. Yellow patterned curtains hung at the window and Betty could see yellow daffodils popping up through the cold earth in the little garden.

*"O*H *I* LOVE ALL *the yellow in this room, it makes it look so warm and friendly."*

Vera smiled.

"Thank you my love. It's my favourite room in the whole house. I love a bit of colour and I often sit over there by the window looking out at the garden. I always put out a bit of bread for the birds, so every day they pop by and I watch them while they have their picnic."

They sat at the little kitchen table to drink their tea. Vera had put the iced doughnuts Betty had brought onto a pretty yellow and white spotted plate and as they ate they chatted happily. It was obvious that the older woman was enjoying having some company.

"How long have you lived here Mrs. Jones?"

"Oh please call me Vera, makes me feel old being called Mrs. Jones."

"Oh, ok Vera."

"Well, I've lived in this house all my life. I was born in the front bedroom upstairs. In those days most babies were born at home. My old grandad built the house, in fact he built all the houses in this street. Well not all on his own of course, he employed quite a few men, but he owned the company. He was still doing building work, just odd jobs mostly, a week before he died when he was 87. I was born in 1931, when Eastbourne was a much smaller place. Of course the town centre was much the same at it is now, most of the houses and shops were built around the same time as this house in the 1800's, but we were surrounded by

countryside and farms then. There was always somewhere nice to go for a walk on a Sunday."

Betty couldn't imagine living in one house for such a long time.

"So you lived here all through the war and everything?"

"Oh yes love. They thought it would be safe here, being just a sleepy seaside town, so hundreds of children were evacuated here from London in 1939. But by 1940 Hitler decided to start bombing us, so things got bad. There was a seafront curfew and they mined the pier in case the enemy tried to land. Of course as kids we thought it was rather exciting, but it must have been jolly hard for our mums and dads, especially with all the rationing and everything. Lots of the local kids ended up being evacuated further out to the country, but mum never let me out of her sight, so I stayed in this house all through the war."

"And you've been here ever since?"

"Yes, I have. I rather thought I'd move out when I got married. I was looking forward to a new adventure. But Herbert said it was best if I stayed here with my parents while he was busy training. So after we got married he travelled around for a few years, just coming home most weekends. He was so ambitious you see, and wanted to wait till he became a bank manager before we settled down properly, bought a house and had a family."

"That must have been really hard for you Vera. Newly married and hardly seeing your husband."

"Yes it was hard. I hated it. But at least I had my mum and dad for company and of course I had a job I loved."

"Where did you work in those days?"

"Oh, at Bobby's, the department store, where I still work. Of course they had to do a lot of rebuilding in the town after the war, after all the bombing, but it was lovely in those days. We'd go

dancing, to the pictures, or the theatre. I met my Herbert at a dance."

Betty heard the catch in her throat as she mentioned her dead husband.

"How old were you when you met him?"

"Oh I was so young. Only nineteen. I hadn't ever had any serious boyfriends, just a few little mild flirtations and when I met Herbert he swept me off my feet. He was a bit older than me, very good looking and charming and so ambitious. I fell for him straight away, but my mum and dad weren't very happy. They didn't think he was right for me. They wanted me to marry a local boy, one of the ones I'd been to school with. But of course in my mind none of those nice young men matched up to the rather sophisticated presence of Herbert."

"So you followed your heart and married him?"

There was a pause.

"Yes. He didn't want to wait, so we got married a year later. But we didn't really live together on our own, properly as husband and wife, for another five years, not until he was promoted to manager at the Seaford branch of the bank, just down the road. Then it was another five years before he got transferred here to the bigger Eastbourne branch. He always said he intended to stay as manager there till he retired. He never expected to die before he got his gold watch and pension."

She sniffed and took a big sip of tea before continuing.

"Once Herbert got his big promotion, he suggested that my mum and dad move to a little flat by the seafront and that we take a cheap bank mortgage and buy them out of the house. I hated the idea, it felt like we were chucking them out of their own home, the only home my mum had ever known. She was born here too you see, back in 1910. But Herbert was very persuasive. He talked about inheritance tax and how we could avoid paying it if they

signed the house over to us. So that's what happened. I think he was the only one who was really happy with the decision. Of course he didn't want to pay the full market price, Herbert was always one to barter, to get a big discount on everything. But at least my mum and dad had a couple of happy years in that flat before they both died. They were just sad that they never had any grandchildren."

"Oh Vera, so you never had any babies? That's so sad."

A few stray tears slid down Vera's face as she replied and she wiped them away with her hand.

"I did have babies, but they all died before they were born. Three little girls and one boy. It was a very sad time. I never thought I'd get over it. But of course time does help. I often think I would have been quite a good mother. Herbert never really minded though, he wasn't as sad as I was. He said children would have probably cost too much and taken up all my time."

BETTY THOUGHT about it as she walked home. What a sad story. It sounded to her as though Vera's husband had not been such a nice man after all. She felt sure her Ian would show a bit more concern if she suffered a tragic miscarriage.

9

DOUBTS CREEP IN

On her way home from work a couple of weeks later, Betty decided to walk along the seafront. It was a lovely evening, so she decided to buy fish and chips for her dinner. It would be a nice little treat after all the stress of the last few weeks.

 It was Andy, the young policeman who had turned up after she discovered the body. He was in the queue for fish and chips too.

"I'm going to sit on that bench and eat mine, why don't you join me?"

They sat in companionable silence for a while, both enjoying their delicious treat and then she told him that she had been visiting Vera.

"She's so lonely without her husband, I feel really sorry for

her. I think she was under his thumb a bit. But at least she still goes to work every day, so she does see people."

*"*ACTUALLY BETTY *I'm really glad I bumped into you today. I wanted to chat to you but couldn't think of a good excuse to contact you. I hope your husband won't mind you being here with me? I've just had a funny feeling since the funeral that something's not right."*

"Oh he won't mind. You are a cop after all, so I'm sure I can trust you."

They both laughed.

"What do you mean about a funny feeling?"

"Well, I know they said at the inquest that it was an accident, misadventure and everything, but I've still got a few questions."

"What kind of questions?"

"Well, for a start, it seems odd that a man who was used to walking home after a few drinks at the pub would suddenly collapse and die, just doing the same thing he'd done hundreds of times before."

"But the coroner said it was an accident."

"I know. It just doesn't quite add up to me. And I overheard a few things at the funeral that made me think."

"What kind of things?"

He went quiet for a few minutes. He really didn't want her to think he was crazy, but he had to talk to someone.

"I tried to tell my boss at the police station, but he told me to keep my mouth shut. That the case was closed and I wouldn't do any good by raking things up."

"What kind of things?"

· · ·

HE CLEARED HIS THROAT.

"Well, you might think I'm mad, over dramatising things, but I've been trained to notice every little thing. So at the funeral, when I sat at the back of the crowded church, I watched how everyone behaved. I was just trying to keep myself amused really. We don't get much in the way of organised crime down here. I'm going to have to get promoted to London or somewhere for that! Of course there are a few criminals here, but we know pretty much who they are. Sometimes I have to escort a prisoner to Lewes Jail, there's lots of wrong-uns in there".

He was aware that he was waffling, trying to impress her.

"ANYWAY, I got to thinking that maybe it wasn't an accident at all, maybe it was murder."

BETTY NEARLY CHOKED ON A CHIP.

"Murder, do you really think so? But surely the police would have thought of that already? They seemed certain it was just an accident."

SHE SHUDDERED, remembering that morning and the shock of seeing the body, frozen under a thick coating of snow.

"WELL, that's what they said, but I think they might be wrong. There's a lot of people round here who didn't like old Mr. Jones. He's upset a lot of people over the years."

.   .   .

"*Oh Andy. I can't believe it. Surely no one would hate him enough to kill him. And there weren't any weapons or anything. He'd only walked home from the pub. You heard that landlady at the funeral. She said that everyone there liked him.*"

"*Not everyone liked him Betty. People always say nice things about the deceased at their funerals. Even if they'd been real bastards when they were alive.*"

"*But his wife Vera is so lovely. I've got to know her pretty well over the last few weeks. Surely she wouldn't have stayed married to him if he'd been a horrible man?*"

He was quiet for a moment, obviously weighing up his words before he spoke.

"*Well actually Betty, I have evidence that he wasn't as nice as people thought he was.*"

"*What kind of evidence?*"

"*Well, admittedly most of it is stuff I've just overheard, but plenty of it can be substantiated. Of course he hasn't got any formal convictions, nothing we can pin on him, not even the odd speeding fine, which is surprising as he used to whizz around those country lanes much faster than the speed limit. He just never got caught. Or at least he was probably let off with a caution. He had lots of connections. But there's plenty of other stuff I found out about him. Being a cop means people often loosen their tongues, particularly if they're trying to even old scores."*

"I DON'T UNDERSTAND *what you mean?"*

"WELL, *for example, there's Maria Finch."*
   "Is she the lady who owns the Italian ice cream shop?"
   "Yes, that's her. "

10

MARIA FINCH

Maria Finch was a well- known figure in the town. Her family owned several businesses: two Italian restaurants, one hairdressers and the ice cream parlour on the sea front.

SHE WAS in her early sixties, a strong formidable woman, still attractive and very outspoken. She had inherited the businesses from her late father, Carlo Bianchi, an ambitious, hardworking man who had come to England when he was in his early twenties. He had bought a little ice cream cart and spent every day dragging it up and down the long beachfront. He had made the ice-cream using an old recipe from his grandmother in Sicily and as there was nothing as exotic already for sale in the town, he had quickly become a great success, gradually expanding his empire. He had borrowed money from the bank and bought freehold property: old run-down buildings on the seafront, which he converted into restaurants, with rooms above for his ever expanding family to live in. By the time he retired, at the age of 83, he was the proud father of six children and grandfather of nine. Together with his beloved wife Sophia, he had created a wonderful legacy.

It had been hard for him at first, a young ambitious man so far from home, whose Italian heritage sometimes made it difficult to be accepted in the rather old fashioned stuffy social circles of the seaside town. So in the 1920's, before he settled down and got married, he changed his name by deed poll to Carlo Finch.

MARIA, his daughter had never married. She had had many offers, in her youth she had been considered one of the most desirable women in the town, but she had never met anyone she felt she could love forever. As a strict Catholic she had no intention of ever having extramarital affairs or divorcing, so it was very important to her that she chose wisely.

She was the eldest daughter in the family and always looked out for her younger sisters.

"ROSA, you must stop seeing this man. He is no good. He will break your heart. And he isn't even a Catholic."

She had begged and pleaded with her sister, to no avail. Rosa thought she was in love and nothing, especially Maria, her bossy older sister, was going to stop her.

"ROSA, please don't do anything silly. Please wait until you get married to give yourself to your husband."

· · ·

BUT OF COURSE Rosa didn't listen. When her parents tried to intervene: to stop her wearing short skirts, staying out late and disobeying their rules, she shouted at them, telling them it was the 1970's, life was changing. No-one stuck to the old rules anymore. This was Eastbourne, not Sicily.

They all despaired. Short of locking her in her bedroom, they didn't know what else to do. Her other siblings were shocked. Apart from Maria, they were all younger, still at school, not yet touched by all the temptations of the modern world.

OF COURSE it all went horribly wrong. At the age of nineteen Rosa found herself pregnant and abandoned by the man who had promised his undying love. He told her that he wasn't ready to be a father and disappeared, fleeing back to his hometown, far away from the wrath of her family. It broke their father's heart. This strong man who had risked everything by leaving his home country to make a good life for his family was broken. He had not been able to protect his baby. He felt a failure, as a man, as a husband and most especially as a father.

Of course the fact that Rosa had kept her boyfriend well away from her disapproving family did not make it easy to find him and after a few years they gave up looking. Her little son Mario flourished in the bosom of her family, but unfortunately Rosa never got over the shame. She became depressed, barely leaving the house, becoming more and more of a recluse as the years passed. She loved her son, but passed over the care of him to her older sister and parents. One day, when the rest of the family were downstairs celebrating the birth of another little cousin, she decided she could go on no longer and hung herself from the staircase.

The family never recovered from the shock. They kept all the businesses going, always putting on a brave face for their customers, but behind closed doors there was always a lingering sadness.

One day, many years later, Maria saw him in the street, the man who had ruined her sisters life. She followed him, thinking that perhaps she was mistaken, after all she hadn't seen him for a long time, surely it was just someone who resembled him. But the minute she heard him speak she knew she was right. His voice was very distinctive. She didn't tell her family, instead over the next few weeks she followed him at every opportunity. She wanted to know everything about him, where he lived, where he worked, who he mixed with.

It came as a shock to discover that he was now a respectable member of the community, a bank manager, a man of some substance. She watched him for months from a distance, watched how he interacted with people. She was very active in the local Business Association, having taken over responsibility for all the family businesses as her father aged. One day she bumped into him at a function and her skin crawled.

"How do you do Miss Finch? Pleasure to meet you. My name is Herbert Jones. I'm your local bank manager. From the big branch in the High Street. Do pop in there anytime, I'm sure there are things we can do which would be beneficial for both our businesses."

. . .

HE WAS JUST as arrogant as she remembered. The man who had ruined her sister's life. She toyed with the idea of confronting him, of grabbing a sharp knife from the buffet table and sticking it in his ribs. But she did nothing. What was the point? Revenge might have been sweet, but it would not bring her sister back. Dragging up the past would just destroy her family, her aged parents might not survive the shock and shame, she would end up in prison for murder and her little nephew, their beloved Mario, would have to live with the public shame of being known as the product of an ill-fated love affair.

So Maria Finch kept her silence. She did not tell Herbert that he had a son, or that her sister had committed suicide because of his ill treatment. She did not tell her parents or any of her siblings that the local bank manager was the man who had destroyed their family. She lived with her grief, but she never forgot.

When she heard that Herbert Henry Jones had died, she went to church, lit a candle and thanked God that her sister could rest in peace at last. And then she went back to her ice cream parlour.

11

____

MORE SUSPECTS

The young policeman had lots more stories to tell Betty.

It seemed he had quite a catalogue of possible suspects, people that he thought carried a grudge against the deceased man. Betty listened carefully.

"WELL, *then of course there's all the people who lost their jobs because of him. He wrecked a lot of lives with his meanness.*"

"I DON'T UNDERSTAND, *what do you mean?*"

"*Well, there's old Mrs Smith for a start. She used to be a secretary at the bank, had been there for years, long before he got transferred there.*"

"SO IS SHE QUITE OLD? *What happened to her?*"

. . .

"*She joined the bank when she was just 18, straight from secretarial college. In those days they used to teach them shorthand as well as typing, so she was well qualified. She'd been there a long time before he arrived and had been really happy. She loved the old bank manager, they worked well together and she was good friends with his wife. She always imagined she'd stay there until she retired.*"

"*You seem to know a lot about her.*"

"*Well actually she's my aunty, my mum's sister, so I know her story well. She used to tell it every Christmas, not realising that we kids were listening. She's one of the reasons I accepted this post. I thought it would be nice to have a bit of family around, I miss my lot up North, especially my mum and dad. I'm actually boarding at my aunties house just off the seafront. She looks after me really well.*"

"*So what happened?*"

"*Well, apparently, her old boss, the nice one with the lovely wife, had a sudden heart attack and had to take early retirement. Then they sent in this new bloke Herbert Jones and he turned the place upside down. Said he wanted a clean sweep and that all the old staff members should think about taking a redundancy package. Of course none of them, including my aunty, wanted to. They liked their jobs, earned good money and wanted to stay as long as possible to make sure they got a full pension when they retired. But in those days bank managers had a bit more power than they do these days. They say he made it difficult for everyone he wanted to get rid of. There were just a couple of young female clerks and the bank messenger that he was happy to keep, he wanted to get rid of the rest of them as soon as possible. Apparently he made it pretty intolerable, and gradually they all resigned. He didn't even have to pay out redundancy to most of them, he just wore them down so they left of their own accord. I don't know the details of course, just the snippets that my aunty told us. But I do know how much he hurt those people, good people who were doing a good job. Of course people have short memories don't they? Most people these days have never heard that story. They just see that smooth bloke in his expensive suits and fancy bow ties swanning about the place, full of his own importance. They have no idea of the misery he's caused so many people."*

"I reckon there's a lot of people who would have danced on his grave if they'd had the chance to."

12

AMY

Amy West had once been passionately in love with Herbert Jones.

Despite now being married to a lovely man: a plumber called Paul who adored her and treated her like a queen, she had never really got over Herbert.

She had been an impressionable young girl when she first met him.

Thrilled to get a job at the local bank, twenty year old Amy had been determined to make her mark, to prove that she was the best secretary the bank had ever employed. She had been top of her class at Pitmans Training College, so her shorthand and typing skills were exemplary and the fact that she was young and pretty sealed the deal.

She had been too young and naïve to realise that her prospective new boss was flirting with her. She had just assumed he was very kind and friendly.

"Well my dear, I think you'll be perfect for the job. Of course I've interviewed several other young ladies, but none of their skills or assets compare to yours. May I suggest you commence your

employment here on the 1st of next month? If you agree, Head Office will be in touch with all the relevant paperwork in the next few days."

IT HAD STARTED out very well. She made sure she was always well dressed, always punctual and friendly with the rest of the bank staff. They were a nice bunch she discovered, very kind and interesting. Ranging in age from the old gentleman Head Cashier who she thought was in his dotage, but in reality had only just turned 60. There were a few middle aged women and a handful of young ones like her. There was even a rather attractive bank messenger called Stuart, who always gave her a winning smile as he left the days mail on her desk.

Her desk was positioned in a small room adjacent to the managers office. She enjoyed going in his office, sitting in that grand wood panelled room on a leather swivel chair, her shorthand book resting on her lap while she waited for him to start dictating his letters.

He was very attractive. It was no hardship to respond to his every beck and call, although two of the other secretaries had tried to warn her to be careful.

"Just watch out for yourself lass. Don't let him overwork you, he's a bit of a tyrant like that. The last girl couldn't take it anymore, headed for a nervous breakdown she was, with all his demands. Oh and don't let him persuade you to stay late, to do any overtime. The last thing you want to do is be alone in the office with him when the rest of us have gone home."

Amy shrugged off all their concerns. She was 20 years old and thought she knew the ways of the world. After all it was 1968, girls of her generation knew much more about things than her mum had done. Young women were burning their bras and even taking that new contraceptive pill to stop having unwanted babies. It was a different world now.

She decided that *she* knew best, so when he started asking her to stay a little late to finish a particular loan application, or type up an important report for Head Office, she was happy to oblige.

During these times he insisted that she sit and work in his office.

"My dear, a pretty young thing like you shouldn't be sitting all alone in that little room, my office is a much better place for you to work. I won't interrupt you, I have a pile of stuff on my desk to deal with. Just let me know when you're done."

ON THE FIRST occasion she had whizzed through the jobs. She didn't really understand why he had insisted they were so urgent, she could easily have got them done in half an hour the following morning. But she was desperate to create a good impression so that he would see what a good worker she was. She really wanted to keep this job.

"I SAY, you are super-fast. Well done. Now I think we should celebrate with a little drink. Sherry ok with you?"

IT BECAME SOMETHING OF A PATTERN. Every couple of weeks he would ask her to stay late, to finish urgent tasks. And every week, once she had completed her work, he poured her a small glass of sherry and asked her about her life.

Amy was thrilled. She was just an ordinary girl who

had lived in the same town all her life. Of course like most young women of her generation, she longed to move to London, to get a trendy flat and to shop in Carnaby Street and the Kings Road, Chelsea. She would get a modern haircut, wear beautiful clothes and date handsome young men.

So it was not altogether surprising that she fell for his charms. He was older, well established and powerful. She had seen the way customers talked to him, he was a man who could change lives, offering bank loans and overdrafts to those in favour and foreclosing on anyone who didn't follow his strict lending rules. In those days, local bank managers had more flexibility, they could decide if a person or business was worthy. She knew that sometimes his decisions were a bit unfair. She had often seen people leave his office in floods of tears following a refusal. She had also seen the way he fawned over developers and other businessmen he admired. They would take him out for an expensive lunch and in the afternoon she would be told to type up overdraft and loan documents. It seemed to her that as long as he fulfilled the financial targets that Head Office set him every month, he was free to make decisions as he saw fit. Of course he was careful, he covered his tracks and ensured that there was never the slightest whiff of bribery about his dealings.

AMY HAD BEEN WORKING for him for two months when he made the first approach. She was totally unprepared, in fact she was a bit cross at being kept late as she had a date that night, with Paul, a handsome young plumber she had met at the local D.I.Y store. She really hoped this wouldn't take too long, as she wanted to get home and change into something a bit more suitable.

"You keep glancing *at your watch Amy. Do you have somewhere you need to be?"*

Afterwards she realised she shouldn't have said anything, it wasn't his business what she did outside work, but she had been brought up to be honest.

"Oh I'm going *on a date. First one with this boy, so I want to go home and change first so I make a good impression."*

She could not believe how slowly he dictated that night. Whereas he would usually rattle through each letter, just giving her a brief outline, knowing she was smart enough to fill in all the gaps, tonight he was agonisingly slow. The clock ticked. Half an hour passed, then an hour. And still he dictated his letters. She wrote as fast as she could, her shorthand really was excellent, but every time he paused, every time she thought he was done, he started up again.

It was 7.30 by the time he let her go. Far too late to go home and change. She would be lucky if she even got to the pub on time to meet Paul. She hoped he wouldn't be too angry.

"Oh Amy, *I don't think it's right him keeping you there all that time. Wasn't there anyone else still working? Does he often make you work late?"*

. . .

SHE COULD TELL Paul was annoyed, so perhaps this wasn't
the right time to tell him how awkward she had felt earlier,
when Mr. Jones had come and perched on the edge of his
desk, his leg uncomfortably close to hers. How he had asked
questions about what she did at the weekend. Did she go
dancing? For the first time in his presence she had felt
uneasy. He was so close that she could smell the alcohol on
his breath, not just the sherry he had insisted on pouring
them both, but also the residue of his liquid lunch. It was a
well-known fact that he popped to the local pub every
lunchtime.

He was so close that she could even see the small pattern
on his red bow tie. He wore a different one every day and all
the bank staff laughed behind his back: it was such an old
man kind of thing to wear. Not very trendy. And apart from
that one thing, Herbert Henry Jones was anything but an old
man. In fact he was rather attractive. But she knew he was
married. She had even met his wife a few times, when she
popped into the bank to pay a bill or withdraw some cash.
She had always seemed lovely, a rather glamorous lady, well
dressed and very charming.

*"OH AMY. You could drive any red blooded man crazy, you are
such a beautiful sexy young woman."*
It was a few weeks later and once again she was stuck in
his office doing overtime.
"Are you still seeing that young man of yours?"
She really didn't want to discuss her love life with her
boss.

"Um no, we broke up. He wanted a girl that would drop everything to see him whenever he wanted to."

"And you didn't want to do that?"

Afterwards she wished she hadn't been so honest.

"Oh he was nice enough, lovely in fact, but I realised we wanted different things. He just wanted a nice easy quiet life, with a wife and kids and a house by the beach."

"And what do you want little Amy?"

She told him about her dream to move to London, to experience all that city life had to offer.

It made it easy to seduce her. Over the course of the next couple of months he ensured that she felt valued. He left flowers and chocolates on her desk after she had worked late. He arranged for her to join him at a few business lunches. Lunches with big development companies who treated them to flashy meals in the best restaurants in town. After working late he took to driving her home in his car. A big flashy, top of the range Jaguar.

"Can't have you hanging around at draughty bus stops my dear, you never know what ruffians might be around."

She had never been treated so well before. And of course it was all perfectly harmless, after all he was her boss and he had a wife.

"ACTUALLY AMY I need to tell you something. I have been putting it off for months, but I can't keep it to myself any longer. I'm falling in love with you."

She was shocked. So shocked that when he put his arm around her she didn't pull away. Instead she took a big gulp from the glass of sherry in front of her.

"But I don't understand? You're married. How can you be in

love with me? I do hope I haven't done anything to encourage you? I've just tried to do my job well."

HE WAS DETERMINED. He spent the next hour making sweet talk, telling her she was the most beautiful creature he had ever seen and that he just had to have her. He was very accomplished, having seduced many women over the years. His position as a bank manager gave him a lot of power.

LATER, Amy often wondered if she should have done more to reject him, but he was relentless. He pursued her for weeks. One evening, when dropping her home after yet another bout of overtime, he leant across to undo her seatbelt and casually brushed his hand against her breast. After that it was easy, he booked a nice hotel, saying it was for a work conference and that he needed her there to take notes.

By the time she had fallen for his charms and had given in to his sexual demands, he was already getting a bit bored. She was cute, young and desperate to please, but there were plenty more fish in the sea for him. Lots of other young women who would be happy to exchange their favours with the bank manager.

"OH HERBERT, you told me you loved me and you were getting a divorce. You said you wanted us to move to London together, to have an exciting life up there. I can't believe you don't want me anymore. I thought we were going to get married and have babies."

· · ·

SHE WAS COMPLETELY HEARTBROKEN. He had promised so much, but obviously had never intended to leave his wife. There was no way she could carry on working with him, so she resigned and took a job at the local D.I.Y store, the same store where she had first met Paul the plumber.

SHE AND PAUL rekindled their relationship. No-one knew about her ill-fated affair with Herbert: well perhaps some of her colleagues at the bank suspected something, but they never mentioned it.

TWENTY YEARS LATER, she was still married to Paul, had three teenage children and a little house by the beach. She was happy, but sometimes wished she could have spent a few years living in a trendy flat in Chelsea.

Occasionally she caught sight of Herbert Jones around the town, but they never spoke.

When she read of his untimely death in the local newspaper she was upset. Not upset because the man she thought she'd once loved had died, but upset because she had never got closure. Never got revenge for all the pain he had caused her. Now she really wished she had been brave enough to confront him, to tell him how much anguish he'd caused her. She had attended his funeral, not to pay her respects, just to make sure he was really gone and could never hurt her, or any other woman again.

13

MORE DOUBTS CREEP IN

It was a small seaside town and in the winter and early spring it was generally pretty quiet. Very few tourists or day-trippers ventured to the chilly seafront and most of the cafes and restaurants were only frequented by locals. This meant there was always lots of gossip flying around. After all, it wasn't every day that someone they knew died. Especially someone as prominent and respectable as the local bank manager.

Tongues wagged.

"Of course, I wouldn't wish a death like that on anyone, imagine freezing to death. But he wasn't my favourite person. I reckon there's plenty of folk in Eastbourne that are glad to see him dead."

"I reckon he deserved it. He was a miserable old so and so."

"I remember when I went to him for a loan, just a small one to tide me over the winter season, just to help till the tourists came

back, and he refused me. Dead arrogant he was, a bit nasty I thought. Gave me a lecture about how I should plan and budget for the quiet times. Spoke to me like I was an idiot. I've been in business since he was still wearing short trousers. Course I switched banks after that, I wasn't going to be talked down to like I was a naughty schoolboy."

"I ALWAYS FELT sorry for that lovely wife of his. She was always so nice and helpful when I went to the store to buy a new dress. But she often seemed a bit sad, I put it down to her losing all those babies, it must have been really difficult for her not having children. Then her mum and dad died and I know that broke her heart too. Mind you, I reckon he was probably a handful, a bit of a demanding baby himself by all accounts. My sister works in that same department store and sometimes she overheard a few things."

"I ALWAYS WONDERED if he was a bit of a womaniser? He seemed to eye up all the women and did you notice that his secretaries were always very young: pretty young things, hardly out of school. He got rid of all the more mature ones, the ones who could do their job well but weren't eye candy for him. Disgusting I call it."

"HAVE you heard all the rumours? They reckon he had a few mistresses around the town. I wouldn't be surprised, I always thought he looked a bit shifty."

. . .

"*MAYBE IT WASN'T an accident after all? Maybe someone did him in, got revenge for his past misdeeds.*"

BETTY WAS COMING to the same conclusion. There was just something suspicious about the whole thing. After all, Herbert had done the same thing every week for many years. There had been nothing unusual about the night he died. Except that it snowed of course. But the snow hadn't started falling till after midnight, long after he should have got home from the pub. It seemed odd that he should have an accident just walking home a few hundred yards, something he had done for years. Still, neither the police or the coroner seemed to think there was anything suspicious. It wasn't as if he had even had a heart attack, they all reckoned he had just banged his head on the concrete path and then frozen to death.

EVERYONE KNEW that he was a regular at the Twitch Arms. The pub was his local, just a five minute walk from his house. He had been frequenting it at least two or three nights a week for the last 20 years. He was well known there and so people often bought him drinks, hoping to curry his favour in case they needed a bank loan in the future. The pub landlady, a peroxide blonde called Cynthia, always made a fuss of him, referring to him as "*that nice Mr. Jones, the bank manager.*"

Of course he was actually something a little more than just her bank manager. Herbert and Cynthia had been having an affair for many years, a secretive clandestine affair carried on virtually under his wife's nose.

Not that Vera ever set foot in the pub. She would have done if he'd invited her to join him: she used to go there often with her mum and dad when she was young, but Herbert told her that it *"wasn't a suitable environment for a delicate flower like you."* This had made her angry, but she had learnt, very early in their marriage, that it was not worth arguing with him about every little thing. It was sometimes much easier just to give in and let him have his own way. But it did make her sad, she had always loved sitting in the pub saloon bar, having a small shandy and a packet of cheese and onion crisps.

CYNTHIA FELT a bit guilty about him cheating on his wife, but she knew it was only a matter of time before he left Vera and moved in to help her run the pub. She had been the land-lady there for fifteen years and it would be nice to have a man about the place.

She had met him years earlier when she went into the bank for a small overdraft, just enough to tide her over the winter months until trade picked up again. He had been very solicitous, giving her lots of advice about balances, spread-sheets and stocktaking and had suggested she make an appointment every three months, so he could check on her progress.

After a couple of visits he had said it would be good for him to inspect the entire pub, just in case she needed further funding in the future for any repairs or alterations. Of course that was the last thing on his mind, it was just an excuse to get her alone, away from prying eyes.

He was a very accomplished lover, having had years of practice with various women and so very soon she was besotted with him. He promised, as men often do, that he was utterly miserable in his marriage, and that as soon as things calmed down he would leave Vera and move in with her. Unfortunately, as he explained on many occasions when she tackled him about the delay, there always seemed to be a problem at home, something that stopped him deserting his wife.

"What kind of man would I be if I left her now, while she's grieving the loss of her parents?"

"I have a lot of problems at work right now my dear. I just need to sort those out and then I'll be free to warm your bed every night."

"Oh Cynthia, she's so heartbroken over all these miscarriages, if I leave her now I'm worried she'll do something silly. She's never been the most stable of personalities. Overly dramatic at the best of times."

Cynthia had listened to all his excuses, getting angrier and more upset as each year passed. On the night he died they had a huge row after closing time, when everyone else had left the pub. Usually this would be the time they went upstairs and made love, but she was sick of him stringing her along. Sick of his excuses.

The last thing she had said to him, as he stormed out of the door, angry that he had been denied his usual sexual relief, were these words. Words that now went around and around in her head.

"I hate you. You've strung me along for all these years. I don't think you're ever going to leave Vera are you? It obviously suits you to seem like a respectable husband even though you've got your bit of stuff on the side. Well, I'm fed up being your bit of stuff. I deserve better. I wish I'd never set eyes on you Herbert Jones. I wish you were dead."

She had cried at his funeral. Cried for the man she loved. Cried for their lost future together. She would do anything to have him back, even if it meant sharing him with his wife. How could she have ever thought she wanted him dead? She kept picturing him lying in the snow, all life gone from him. His dead eyes and the coating of snow on his moustache and bushy eyebrows. His lips, so pale and cold.

14

FLORENCE

"*I hated that man. I'm really glad he's dead. At least now he won't be able to hurt anyone else.*"

Her family were shocked. They had never heard Florence talk so hatefully about someone before.

SHE WAS a sensible middle aged woman, a loving wife and mother of three teenage daughters. Daughters who were sometimes frustrated by her fierce protectiveness.

"*Mum, that's not very nice. I've never heard you speak like that before.*"

It was true.

Florence was the nicest of women, a kind gentle soul who would do anything for anybody.

"*Now come on girls, leave your mum alone. She doesn't have to like everyone. I'm sure she's got her reasons for talking like that.*"

Later that night, when all three girls were tucked up in

their beds, reading their library books or listening to the latest pop songs on their transistor radios, Florence's husband Jim spoke.

"Love, whatever's wrong? I've never heard you talk so harshly about anyone before. Me and the girls were quite shocked. I didn't even realise you knew that bloke, let alone had such strong feelings about him."

"It's not something I'm proud of and I never meant to blurt it out like that, especially in front of the girls."

They were both silent for a while.

"But I suppose I'd better tell you now. Tell you why I'm so glad he's gone."

It turned out that Florence was another of Herberts conquests at the bank.

She had hated him for years.

"I WAS JUST 17, straight from typing college when I got the job at the bank. I was so happy. It was a real step up in the world for me, an ordinary girl from the council estate. I loved that job. My first boss, old Mr. Grimes, was lovely, a real gentleman. He was so kind to us all, treated us really well. Then after I'd been working there for a year, he had a heart attack and had to retire and we got this new young manager, Herbert Jones. At first us girls were really happy. He was charming and good looking and he seemed to really appreciate our work. There were six of us secretaries working there then. Then gradually he got rid of all the older, more mature ladies. At first we thought they wanted to leave, but then we realised he was targeting them, making their lives intolerable, so intolerable that in the end they resigned rather than put up with it anymore. Of course in those days it was harder for women. If we complained, men would shout us down, saying we *were lucky to have a job when we should really be at home, minding the house and children. And of course we earned much less than them, even those women that were doing exactly the same jobs. It was a different time. I'm not sure men like him could get away with that kind of behaviour now."*

Her husband was shocked. She was visibly upset. Whatever would she say next?

"Anyway, it all kicked off at the staff Christmas party. There were a lot of us there, current staff, old ones and a handful of partners. I didn't have a boyfriend then, so I'd gone on my own. Mr. Jones was on his own too, he explained that his wife Vera was very disappointed not to be there, but that she was suffering from a dreadful migraine, so was stuck at home."

Sally, a feisty blonde twenty year old from accounts, had scoffed at this, she reckoned she had seen Vera that very afternoon, looking fit as a fiddle working in the department store.

"I reckon he just wants all us beauties to himself tonight, he doesn't want his wife here keeping her beady eye on him, making sure he behaves himself."

Of course they had all dressed up. It was the one night in the year, apart from New Year's Eve of course, when they could get dolled up. Tonight Florence was wearing her absolute favourite dress, a floor-length figure hugging dress in a pink sparkly Lurex fabric. She knew it suited her, so she felt very pretty and confident. Sally was wearing a very short tight-fitting dress in black velvet. Both girls were young and pretty, with good figures, so they had no shortage of male attention.

"Good evening Florence. You are looking exceedingly beautiful tonight. I almost didn't recognise you out of your usual office attire. I must say this is a huge improvement. Stunning in fact."

She was rather lost for words.

"Oh thank you sir. And thank you for throwing us this lovely party. We are all having such a good time. It's such fun. The music's great and this food is delicious. I love the cheese and pineapple on sticks and the prawn vol au vents."

She knew she was warbling, but it made her rather uncomfortable seeing the way his eyes were roaming over her body.

He insisted that she dance with him. Apparently he felt it was his duty to dance with all his female employees.

"Oh I don't need another drink thank you sir. I've already had a couple. I don't want to get tipsy."

"Nonsense, another little one won't hurt you, here have this."

She was vaguely aware that each time he insisted on another dance, he also handed her another drink. At first she thought it was just the same one each time, but she realised her error when she began to feel giddy, almost as though she was going to faint.

"Come and sit down in my office. Someone might bump into you on the dance floor, it's getting a bit wild out here. Soon be time for me to send everyone home I think. They'll be a few sore heads in the morning. Good job it's Saturday tomorrow so they won't have to come into work."

Florence, that sweet innocent young woman, had no idea of his intentions. She was still a virgin. Of course there had been several young men who had tried to seduce her before, but they did not have the charm, experience, or power that Herbert Jones had.

She tried to fight him off, but he was stronger than her.

His office door was firmly closed, so no-one at the party could hear her as she begged and pleaded with him.

It was over quickly and as he stood up and got dressed he looked down at the sobbing young girl.

"Oh don't make a fuss girl. If you dress like that you're just asking for it. Don't tell me you didn't want it. Hurry up and get dressed. The others will be wondering where we got to."

Florence never went back to the party. Instead she got dressed and left by the back door, hailing a taxi to take her to the safety of her own home, her own family.

On the following Monday morning she walked into the bank, collected her coat and handbag, which had been left behind the other night in her despair, and handed in her resignation. She noticed the pitying glances from some of her colleagues as she left the building. Obviously her rape and assault had not gone completely unnoticed, he had probably done it before.

FLORENCE ONLY TOLD HER MUM. Her dad would have gone marching into the bank, demanding the managers blood and she knew that it would do no good. No-one would take the word of a girl from the rough council estate over that of a respectable bank manager.

It took her many years to get over it, to put aside the shame and anger. Her friend Sally turned up one day and mentioned it out of the blue.

"I guessed that's what happened. That bastard had got away with it again. I know of at least four girls he's done it to. At least you didn't get pregnant."

. . .

JIM, Florence's husband, was utterly distraught.

"*Oh Flo, I wished you'd told me. Now I understand why you didn't date much before we met. You must have been terrified of it happening again. I realise now why you're so protective of our girls, not wanting them to get hurt like you were. What a bastard. I'm glad he's dead. Otherwise I'd have to go and kill him myself.*"

15

JONATHON WEST (BABY-WEAR SHOP OWNER)

onathon West was a rather timid young man.

He came from a very wealthy family, an old established family in the town and he was the youngest of six children. *"The runt of the litter"* his father always called him.

He was kind, gentle and a little too fond of reading and music as far as his brothers and father were concerned. They much preferred sports: rugby, cricket, hunting and fishing. The last thing they wanted to do was sit quietly and read, or listen to classical music. If they couldn't be out showing off their manly prowess on the sports field, they preferred to bed as many women as possible. Because they were rich and had considerable social standing in the town, this was never a problem, there were always queues of willing young women, hoping for a life of idle, carefree riches.

Jonathon was very different to his brothers. He was still a virgin at the age of 23, by choice. It wasn't that he was a prude, he liked women, in fact he liked them much better than most men did, but he had never found anyone he wanted to settle down with. He didn't just want a pretty girl, he wanted someone he could have decent conversations with, someone who was interested in books, travel and adventure. Not the kind of adventures his brothers liked: mountaineering, skiing, deep sea diving and dangerous water sports, but more gentle adventures: exploring the world, discovering ancient civilisations, going to concerts and book signings. He realised that most modern young women didn't share his tastes, it seemed they were more interested in the latest fashions and make up, pop stars, fast cars and beach holidays. He hated the beach, hated the way the sand stuck to his feet and the hot rays turned his body a fetching shade of lobster. His brothers of course all had olive skin, inherited from their Greek father, and tanned beautifully, while poor Jonathon had got his skin tone from his mother, a beautiful fair skinned redheaded Irish heiress. She of course adored him, her baby, the one who was most like her in both looks and temperament.

She was the one who protected him at all costs. Protected him from his loud overbearing brothers, his rather critical father and all the unsuitable young ladies who flocked around, hoping to snag a rich husband.

By the time he was 18, his brothers had all left home, had successful careers, were married and had produced a few children. Jonathon was the only one remaining in the family home.

"What is wrong with that boy? He didn't want to go to university, doesn't seem to have many friends and can't hold down a decent job. I despair. He doesn't even seem to have any girlfriends. There's plenty of nice young women around here he could settle down with. Perhaps he bats for the other team? I damn well hope not. How would we ever live down the shame? I

had an old uncle like that and he was sent out to live in Africa. Never came home again. No-one in the family ever talked about him, except in hushed tones. Of course in those days homosexuality was a crime."

His father didn't realise that Jonathon was in the next room and could hear every word.

"Oh my dear, don't be so hard on the boy. Just because he's not a James Bond type like his brothers doesn't mean he's less of a man. You know how kind and sensitive he is, would do anything for anybody. He just hasn't quite found his place in life yet, but he will, mark my words. We just have to be patient and understanding."

As always his mother was defending him.

Just a few weeks later he was working in his uncle's restaurant and he met her. The woman who was to become his wife.

It was the most upmarket restaurant in town, expensive and exclusive. His uncle was a fairly well known chef, so although he was rarely in residence, people flocked there, hoping to catch sight of or even meet the great man. Jonathon found this rather amusing. He loved his uncle, but was well aware that despite his minor celebrity status, he was actually now something of a recluse, preferring to spend his time climbing mountains in Austria rather than entertaining dinner guests.

Jonathon worked as front of house, his good looks and quiet cultured manner made him very suitable for such a position.

He noticed her the minute she walked in. It was obviously an office party, not raucous but lively. A group of seven people, four men and three young women, all beautifully dressed and obviously excited to be dining in such a grand establishment.

"Good evening. Welcome to Phillipe's restaurant. We are delighted to have you with us this evening. May I offer you a complimentary cocktail?"

He knew that people appreciated this little touch, it made them feel welcome and rather special. His uncle was very clever.

"Is Monsieur Phillipe in the kitchen this evening? We have heard so much about his cooking and can't wait to meet him."

The pretty girl in the shiny red dress spoke. The girl he had noticed as soon as she walked in the door.

"I am so sorry. My uncle is away at the moment, travelling in Europe. But he has trained all the chefs here, so I am sure you will not be disappointed."

"Your uncle is Phillipe? Are you French too? You don't have an accent."

Jonathon groaned inwardly. Of course his uncle wasn't French at all and his name was actually Philip, not Phillipe, but he had decided early on in his cooking career that people thought anyone from France was a better cook. Now it had become part of his persona and as he was constantly travelling, barely seen in person at his restaurant, it was up to his staff to keep up the pretence.

"No, I was born here, although my father is Greek and my mother Irish."

He had found that was sufficiently exotic to satisfy most people in the absence of his elusive uncle.

"Oh okay. Well I'm disappointed we won't meet the great man himself, but I'm sure you'll look after us beautifully."

She looked up at him with a winning smile.

He couldn't take his eyes off her all evening. She was so vivacious, constantly talking and making her fellow diners laugh. Every time he went to their table to check whether they needed anything, she smiled at him, smiles that made him feel rather weak at the knees.

As they left the restaurant, after splitting the rather large bill between the seven of them, he made a point of handing her his business card.

JONATHON WEST.
  Phillipe's Restaurant.
  The Meads.
  Eastbourne.
  Tel: 7615432

HE NEVER EXPECTED her to call, but she did, the very next day.

Within a week he was hooked. Felicity Green, the girl in the red dress, was the kind of woman who knew exactly how to ensnare a man.

He took her out every night when he wasn't working, to flashy restaurants and clubs. He knew she was the kind of woman who expected such treatment. He always insisted on paying the whole bill, he was far too much of a gentleman to expect her to pay anything.

He always picked her up in his brand new top of the range sports car that his parents had given him for his 21st birthday.

She lived in the Old Town, an established area full of large houses quite near to the seafront. He had assumed that she lived with her parents in the rather splendid brick mansion, and was a little surprised a few weeks later when she let slip that actually she just rented a room there, sharing the facilities with ten other people. But by then he didn't care, it wouldn't have mattered to him if she had just stepped off an alien spaceship, he was truly besotted with her, his first love.

He proposed after just three months, terrified that if he didn't snap her up, someone more eligible would. He had no idea that she was marrying him for his money, he truly believed her when she said that she had fallen passionately in love with him and couldn't wait to become his wife.

Their wedding was a pretty grand affair. In the end he and his parents had paid for everything, after she had tearfully confessed that actually she had been estranged from her parents for the last five years and that they wouldn't be coming to the wedding.

It had torn at his heartstrings, how on earth could anybody, especially her own family, not care about this lovely woman.

She made a beautiful bride of course. Her dress, made of satin and lace, came from the best bridal boutique, her shoes were handmade and her enormous bouquet had been designed by a renowned florist. It was a shame there were only a handful of people on her side of the church, just her close friends and work colleagues, not a relative in sight, but Jonathon vowed that he would always be by her side, ensuring she would never be lonely again.

They honeymooned in the Maldives. It was hugely expensive, but he knew she loved being pampered, so he was happy to give up most of his savings to keep his new bride happy.

. . .

THE FIRST FEW months of their married life passed quickly. He was still working in his uncle's restaurant and she continued with her office job. They visited his parents every Sunday, enjoying a huge roast dinner, washed down with expensive wine from his fathers cellar. He noticed that she was always more animated on those occasions. Often at home in his bachelor apartment on the seafront, he would catch her gazing wistfully out of the window.

"Jonathon, do you think we could move? I don't like living here much. I think it's time we bought a house, started to build a nest together."

He would have done anything to please her. So the very next weekend she dragged him around open homes, looking at houses. Not just any houses: the kind of place you would expect newly married couples to begin their lives in, but big executive homes. Brand new, with four bedrooms, ensuite bathrooms, offices, laundry rooms and big gardens.

"Oh Felicity darling, don't you think they're a bit more than we need right now? After all there's only the two of us. We'd rattle around in something as big as that."

"But Jonathon, I thought you wanted a family."

"Oh darling of course I do, you know that. I'd love at least four children. But not yet. I'd really like to have you to myself for a bit longer. After all, I've only known you for a year. We're young, surely we can wait a couple more years before we try for a baby. It would be nice to do some travelling first. I've always wanted to see more of Italy and perhaps even venture as far afield as Bali and Singapore. I've got an auntie who lives in New Zealand, so I've always fancied going there too."

But Felicity had no intention of waiting. She wanted a baby and a big house now!

Six months later she was pregnant and standing in the kitchen of their new home: a large detached house in the most exclusive street in town.

The money he got from selling his apartment had barely covered the deposit on the new one, so he had borrowed the rest from the bank.

"I think we should upgrade the kitchen. This one is looking rather shabby. I've seen one I like in the latest Homes and Gardens magazine. Also, I'm fed up with you being out every night working in that restaurant. I think we should start a business together."

"Oh darling, I'm not sure that's a good idea. We don't really have any business experience. What on earth could we do?"

"Well actually Jonathon, I've found the ideal business for us. It's just come on the market. Here, in Eastbourne. Old Mr. White is selling his baby-wear business on the High Street. It's in a great position, right opposite the bank and the supermarket, so there's lots of foot traffic"

"Selling baby-wear? Really? Whatever makes you think we'd enjoy doing that? I like working in the restaurant, can't see myself standing around selling prams and baby clothes all day."

It was not often that Jonathon stood up to his wife. He had gone along with her plan to buy a new house, and never complained when the credit card bill came in every month about her exorbitant spending. But this was different. This would affect his whole life.

"But what about the baby. Surely you won't be able to work once he or she comes along?"

"Oh don't be ridiculous Jonathon, a baby-wear shop is the perfect environment to bring a baby up in. We'll have our pick of

all the best equipment, I daresay we'll even be able to persuade the manufacturers to give us a free pram and car seat, it'll be good advertising for them."

He had been most reluctant at first, but after speaking to his father, who assured him that *"a happy wife means a happy life"* he went against his better judgement and took out yet another hefty bank loan to buy the shop and all its stock.

Their baby, a little girl who Felicity insisted on calling Grace, after Jonathon's recently deceased grandmother, became the light of his life. She seemed to care about him more than his wife, who had become a little distant following the birth of their daughter. At first he had just put it down to post-natal depression: his mother had explained to him that it was common among new mothers and that he should give his wife space to recover.

When baby Grace turned five, it was obvious to Jonathon and his parents that they had outlived their usefulness. They had provided Felicity with a lovely wedding, a loving family and a fine home and thriving business. In return she treated them all with disdain.

"I have provided you with an heir, a daughter you adore. Now it's time for me to have a bit of fun. I'm fed up being stuck here, in this boring town, running this boring business. I want more from life."

She started to stay out late, pretending she was going out with her girlfriends and old work colleagues. Jonathon became suspicious. She would often get home after midnight, seemingly unconcerned as to the welfare of her husband and small daughter.

Then the rumours started. Eastbourne was a small place. All the shopkeepers knew each other. He overheard things.

"Of course that poor man has no idea how she carries on. I

saw her, with my own eyes, staggering out of the pub last week, draped round that handsome young man who works in the Insurance office."

"Oh I saw her last night, at that nice pub at East Dean. You know, the one on the Green. She was tucked away in a quiet corner, snuggled up with that bank manager, Mr. Jones. I was very surprised to see them there. They're both married. Of course that pub is a good place to carry on an affair, especially in the winter when its quiet and there aren't lots of tourists around."

He tried to turn a blind eye. Hopefully if he didn't make a fuss she would soon come to her senses. He knew she found him boring, but he had hoped that running a business together would make them grow closer. Instead it seemed to have done quite the opposite.

In the end, he could be quiet no longer.

"Felicity, please stop seeing that man. People are talking. He's married, just think how his wife would feel if she found out."

She had laughed in his face.

"Herbert is a far better man than you'll ever be Jonathon. He listens to me, he understands me. And he's a good lover. He's going to tell his wife this weekend that it's over, that he wants a divorce and is going to marry me. We thought we'd move to Spain."

Of course Herbert Henry Jones had absolutely no intention of ever leaving his wife. It suited him very well to have a quiet obliging little woman at home, leaving him to pursue other conquests whenever the inclination overcame him.

FELICITY WAS HEARTBROKEN. She had truly believed that he loved her and intended taking her away from all this, to another sunnier more exciting life. Gossip travels fast in a small place and when she found out he was also seeing the pub landlady and his young secretary, she was incandescent with rage. She said nothing to Herbert. She could not trust herself. She just wanted to put her hands around his neck and strangle him. She took her anger out on her husband instead.

"Ok Jonathon. I'm done. I can't stay here any longer. Not in this boring place, doing this boring job. I am flying to Spain next week and taking Grace with me. You can come and visit her there of course. My solicitor will be in touch."

Jonathon was completely heartbroken. He turned to drink, stopped paying the mortgages on both the house and the business and the bank foreclosed on his loans. The bank manager came to pick up the keys to the shop.

"Oh dear, old chap. Such a shame your wife left you in the lurch. These women do play with our emotions don't they. But I'm sure your parents will help you out won't they?"

Jonathon could not respond. How dare this wretch of a man, the man responsible for destroying his marriage and sending away his wife and daughter, talk to him like that. Obviously he didn't realise that he knew about the affair. Or maybe he just didn't care.

On the day he heard that Herbert Henry Jones had frozen to death, Jonathon began to live again. At last that dreadful man had got his just desserts. He rather enjoyed thinking about his dead body covered in snow, he just hoped the man had really suffered before he lost consciousness.

16

JIMMY THE BANK MESSENGER

The sun seemed to shine every day after the funeral. Suddenly it seemed as though the world was a better place. Everywhere Jimmy looked he saw joy. Joy at the warmth from the sun on people's faces after the long cold winter. Joy on the faces of the children running along the beach. Joy on the faces of the old folk sitting outside eating their Pensioners Special fish and chips. Joy everywhere.

He felt pretty joyful too. He no longer dreaded going in to work every day. Now there would be no more humiliation, no more pent up anger.

He had danced around the kitchen in his little flat on the day he heard that Herbert Jones had died. Herbert Jones, his boss, the man who humiliated him every day.

Jimmy had been just 17 years old when he got the job at the bank. He had been thrilled, at last he had an opportunity to prove himself, to prove to the world that he was worth something.

He had been born with a cleft lip and one leg much

shorter than the other. His young unmarried mother had taken one glance at her not quite perfect baby and decided she could not bear to look after him. So he had been handed over to the local authority, who after trying unsuccessfully for a couple of years to find adoptive parents for him, had given up and placed him in a children's home. Jimmy never really knew any other life, so was fairly content. Of course it hurt him when he started school and the other kids teased and bullied him about his appearance. Although he had been given a cleft palate operation when he was tiny, his unusual look, slight speech impediment and built up shoe to correct his gait, made him an easy target.

"Peg leg."

"Wonky Jimmy."

"Orphan boy."

Some of the insults were much worse, but he did his best to ignore them. He was a very kind and affectionate boy, a good student, diligent and hardworking, and after a few years he had earned the respect of his teachers and even some of the bullies. Everyone at the children's home loved him too and so his childhood was fairly happy. Every Sunday the children would march, crocodile style, down to the seafront to the Italian ice-cream shop, where they would be treated to delicious ice-cream cornets, supplied for free. Old Mr. Bianchi (Maria Finches father) had started this tradition back in the 1930's.

He understood loneliness and poverty. When he had first arrived in Eastbourne as a young man, with no friends, no family, no money and no job, he used to sit on the seafront every Sunday after attending mass at the local Catholic church. He would watch the line of orphan children as they marched down to the stoney beach, then smile as they ran around, free as little birds, enjoying the fresh sea air. He noticed the sad looks on their faces as they saw other children enjoying ice-creams bought by their indulgent parents from the little kiosk on the pier. At those moments he knew he wanted to make a small difference to the lives of those poor abandoned children. So, years later, as soon as he had established his first ice cream shop, he went to the children's home and made his offer. Since then, every single Sunday, rain or shine, he and his staff had made the biggest, best and most delicious ice cream cornets for every kid who passed through that home. Even after the old man died, the tradition continued.

Jimmy and his friends were the last inhabitants of that children's home. After receiving a very generous offer for the house and land (some two acres in all) it closed its doors for the final time. A greedy developer then built ten large executive homes on the site and the children were despatched elsewhere.

Jimmy had just turned 16, so he knew he would have to leave there eventually, but it still broke his heart. To say goodbye to the other kids, his carers and the only real home he had ever known was a wrench. He was put into a hostel, along with a couple of his mates and they all hated it. They were the youngest there, most of the other residents were hardened men. Some like them, had grown up in the care system, others had taken the wrong path in life and become drunkards, addicts, or criminals. It was a very unhealthy environment for three vulnerable boys, so eventually they were moved out and placed in a council run housing block, where they each had their own bedroom and shared kitchen and bathroom facilities with the other tenants. It was more like the home environment they had been used to all their lives. There was a cleaner, a cook and a careers advisor/father figure/house leader on site and after a while they settled in and enjoyed their new found freedom. It was just a stone's throw to the beach, you could hear the seagulls squawking as soon as you opened the windows and Jimmy loved it.

"Okay lads. Time we found you some jobs."

Old Bill, their house leader spoke gently. He too had been an orphan, and knew that these boys, despite their air of bravado, were terrified, suddenly out in the big world alone, with no-one to support them.

It was his job to get them sorted out, to give them some life skills, to teach them how to live in this crazy world that they had been sheltered from for so long.

"But Bill, can't we just carry on at school? Mikey wants to be an engineer and Jimmy really wants to go to university or teachers training college. I don't care, I just want to be a mechanic, so any old apprenticeship in a garage would suit me, but them two are really smart, it would be a shame to waste such good brains."

Terry spoke with passion. The three boys had been firm friends since the age of three. All abandoned by families who didn't want them, they had formed an incredibly strong bond, a bond that would last all their lives.

"Oh lads. I really wish I could wave a magic wand and give you the lives you deserve, but I'm afraid my hands are tied. The Council will pay for a bit of training, just to get you started, but I'm afraid there's no chance of further education. They've cut all the grants you see. But I've done the best I can. So you Terry, can start at the Ford dealership next week. Old Ted who owns it is a mate of mine and he's promised to train you well, give you a proper mechanics apprenticeship and all."

Terry beamed.

"Frank, I've managed to get you a job at the Rodmell Cement Works.

I know you'd set your heart on becoming an engineer, but that takes years and an awful lot of training and studying. I reckon if you keep your head down and work hard you'll do well there."

"AND JIMMY. I'm really sorry lad that I can't swing it for you to carry on with your education. You're a smart lad and would go far if you got a university degree, but I'm afraid that's just not possible. The council say there's no scholarships available. But you could always do some evening classes, they don't cost much. Anyway, I've managed to get you a position at the local bank."

For a moment Jimmys heart soared. The bank! A chance to prove himself, to show that he wasn't just a dumb crippled boy from the children's home. But Bills next words destroyed that dream.

"You are going to be one of the bank messengers. You'll be working under my mate Stuart, he's a great bloke."

"But what will I do there? What is a bank messenger?"

"Oh it's a very important job. In a big branch of the bank like we have here in town, there are always jobs to be done, errands to run, things to sort out. Stuart will explain it all to you. He's been there for years."

"Oh and by the way, the Council have agreed that you can all stay here for as long as you like, they'll just charge you a bit for rent and board once you start working."

AND SO, some ten years later, Jimmy was still living in that house and still working at the bank. The job had turned out better than he expected. People were kind to him, none of the other staff teased him about his slightly disfigured face or crooked leg, they were just grateful that he was such a good hardworking man, someone who didn't mind how many demands they asked of him. Jimmy became well known and well-loved for his sunny nature and winning smile.

All was well in Jimmy's life until the arrival of the new bank manager, Herbert Henry Jones.

Herbert Jones was arrogant, self-opinionated and rather cruel. He was totally the opposite of the old manager.

Over the course of the next few years Jimmy studied him carefully. As the bank messenger: the only one now, as Stuart had taken early retirement a couple of years earlier after being abused verbally once too often by Herbert.

Jimmy didn't mind having to do the work of two men, in fact he enjoyed the challenge. He didn't have much else going on in his life, his two mates had moved out and got married and although the other blokes in the house were nice enough, he didn't have much rapport with them. He, Terry and Frank would meet up every Friday night for a few drinks after work and reminisce about old times, but he could sense them gradually slipping away to their new lives, to their wives and now children. He was proud to have been asked to be god-father to them all: little Hetty, Alice and James were the light of his life. He knew he would probably never have a wife or children of his own. Women just didn't seem to find him attractive.

THE PROBLEMS at work had started pretty much straight away. As soon as Herbert Jones took over the managers position. Until then it had been a really happy working environment, everyone had got on well and treated each other with respect. They had all gone out for drinks after work once a month on payday, and the old manager had always insisted on buying the first round. He knew how to treat his staff properly. But somehow Herbert changed all that. Within a few weeks there were cracks forming. He sacked all the older female staff, offering them small redundancy packages, but making it quite clear that as they were now surplus to requirements, he would find a way of getting rid of them if they didn't agree to leave voluntarily.

Jimmy knew this wasn't fair. Those women had been loyal hard workers, some for more than 20 years and now this new chap was chucking them out like they were dirt on his shiny shoes. He wondered if he should complain to Head Office, he was absolutely sure they didn't know what was going on. He didn't know how Herbert expected to get away with it, it wasn't his decision as to who was offered redundancy and who wasn't, those kind of decisions always came from above.

But, somehow Herbert got his way. Four secretaries, all over the age of forty five, tearfully handed in their notices and cried bitter tears at the leaving party held in the pub on their final payday. The next day Maisie the cleaner handed in her notice too, announcing that she couldn't work for that *"nasty grasping bloke a moment longer."*

Jimmy was sad to see Maisie go. She had always been such a good friend to him, right from the day he had first started working there as a shy, socially awkward boy. He had blossomed under the caring eye of her and the old manager. She had always had time to chat, leaning on her mop or vacuum cleaner, giving him the benefit of her wisdom and always sneaking him a couple of extra digestive biscuits with his cup of tea. He would really miss her.

"Oh Maisie, I know he's a nasty bit of work, but couldn't you reconsider. It won't be the same here without you."

"Oh Jimmy love. Course I'll miss you too. I love seeing your smiley face every day, but I just can't stand it anymore. Mind you I'll really miss the money. And the company. I'm going to try and get a job in that new superstore that's opening up near the station. It's a big place so I reckon they'll be needing a few experienced cleaners. And I can walk there every day, don't want to take a job where I have to catch the bus to work."

She didn't tell him that she was leaving not just because Herbert was difficult to work for, but because she had seen the way he treated people. Not just the women who worked in the bank, the women he could pester with sexual advances and then dismiss if they didn't agree to his demands, but also the female bank customers. She had seen several women leaving his office in a state of distress and knew the reason. For some reason people seemed to think the cleaners were invisible, but Maisie had seen many things that distressed her greatly. He hadn't tried anything on with her yet, but she knew it was probably just a matter of time. The man had no morals or scruples, and according to her friend Elizabeth, who worked in the pub where he went for his lunch every day, he behaved badly there too, using his social standing as an excuse to treat women with less respect than they deserved. There were plenty of rumours flying around the town about his behaviour. Maisie just felt sorry for that wife of his, she seemed like such a nice lady.

·   ·   ·

THE YEARS PASSED and Jimmy got to hate Herbert Jones more and more. He hated the way he treated women with disdain. Hated the way he spoke down to everybody, it was like he considered himself a greater being, someone who didn't need to behave with common decency. Jimmy had never really hated anyone in his whole life before. He was a gentle soul, kindness personified, and he hated injustice of any kind. But he hated Herbert Henry Jones with a passion and was delighted to hear of his untimely death. It had always rather surprised him that no-one had ever murdered the bloke before now, there were enough people in the town that had a grudge against him. Still, now they could all be free, free from the clutches of that truly unpleasant man. Of course Jimmy felt sad for his widow Vera, she was a lovely woman, far too good for that dreadful man, in his opinion. Hopefully in time she would get over her loss, find a decent man and marry again.

Jimmy just wished he could have been brave enough to finish the bloke off years ago. That would have saved a lot of pain and misery for so many people.

17

SIMON BLOW (THE UNDERTAKER)

Simon Blow was an unusual character. He had wanted to be an undertaker since he was five years old. His mother had been upset when he first mentioned it, but dismissed it as a childish fantasy.

"Mum, that's what I want to do when I grow up. Wear a black suit and a top hat, have a couple of horses with feathers and a big car to carry the dead people around in."

He never changed his mind. The schools career officer was horrified when he announced at the age of 15, that he wasn't in the least bit interested in becoming a policeman, a fireman or a footballer like the rest of the boys in his class. No, he still wanted to be an undertaker.

So, on his 16th birthday he started his apprenticeship at Joshua Bloom Undertakers, an old established funeral business. Joshua Bloom The Third, great grandson of the original owner, was absolutely delighted to have a young man keen to learn the profession, it was hard to attract staff normally and the rest of his workforce was approaching retirement.

Their premises were down a brick alleyway, just off the High Street. An alleyway just wide enough to accommodate a horse and carriage, but a little tight for large modern hearses. They often had to do little paint touch ups where the cars had inadvertently scraped against the brick walls.

The offices themselves were very old, Dickensian even, with old wooden desks and chairs, fake flowers and coffins and urns displayed in every nook and cranny. Simon was enchanted. It was everything he had imagined a proper undertakers place to be.

He worked diligently, loving every moment. It didn't faze him to see all the dead bodies, somehow he felt more comfortable with them than with living people. He could have a nice chat as he made them presentable for their families to view. It didn't matter that they didn't reply. He really felt he had found his life's work, the vocation he was always intended to do. He became a great asset to the business, always willing to help in any way he could, staying late if necessary, even doing weekend and night work if they had a lot of funerals to prepare for.

He was such an asset that twenty years later, when old Mr. Bloom wanted to take part time retirement, he offered Simon a partnership, a fifty percent share of the business. Simon was absolutely thrilled.

"AND WHAT CAN I do for you today young man?"

The bank manager was rather pompous, but Simon spoke confidently, explaining his case clearly and concisely.

"Well, I've been offered a share in the funeral business. You know, Bloom and Co. just round the corner. And I wondered if you could give me a loan. I've got some savings, but not enough."

"How much do you need?"

"Five thousand pounds please."

"Five thousand, that seems rather cheap for a share in such a lucrative business. How much is old Bloom charging you altogether?"

"Oh, I already have five thousand of my own, I just need another five thousand. He's letting me have a share for much less than it's worth, I've been working there for more than twenty years you see, since I was sixteen."

DESPITE HIS ARROGANT MANNER, Herbert Jones recognised a good risk when he saw it, this young man was clearly capable and honest. But why should he make it easy for him, no-one had ever given himself, Herbert, anything for nothing, certainly nothing as valuable as a share in a thriving business.

"WELL OF COURSE THE Bank can't just lend money willy nilly to anyone who walks in off the street. That would be most irresponsible. What qualifications do you have for running a business, have you ever done an accounting course or anything of that sort? How much input would old Bloom still have in the business? Is he planning on retiring or will he still have his hands on the reins? Do you understand about tax liability, profit and loss, end of year accounts? Do you know how much all the stock costs, coffins and the like? There's more to running a business than just putting on a dark suit and charming the mourners you know."

Simon was furious. How dare that dreadful man talk down to him like that. But he needed the loan, so he had to be polite and not show his anger.

· · ·

In the end, terms were agreed. More favourable to the bank than Simon of course, but he didn't care. At last he would be a real undertaker.

Six months later the doorbell tinkled and he looked up from his desk, ready to greet his customers. He was very surprised to see Herbert Jones standing there. He had not set eyes on the man since he went into the bank to sign the final loan documents.

"Oh Good Morning Mr. Jones. How are you sir?"

"In a rush, got an important meeting to go to, but need you to organise a couple of funerals for me."

"Oh I'm so sorry for your loss. Were they close family?"

Simon already knew who they were, but he wasn't going to let on. It was the talk of the town. That poor elderly couple, dying within hours of each other in their little seafront flat. Rumour was that it was down to a leaky gas heater or something. Their landlord should be taken to court. Disgusting to take decent peoples money and then give them a shoddy place to live.

"My wife's parents. She's devastated of course. So I said I'd take over all the arrangements, to save her the worry. She'll want to pop in of course, to view them once you've tidied up the bodies. So, I want your very best. The best coffins, the best flowers, walking in front of the hearse all the way to the church and all of that. Oh and I suppose we'll need a bit of a do afterwards, lets book the Grand Hotel for that, I know the general manager there,

so just mention my name and he'll do a good deal. Allow for about 50 guests. They've finished the inquest now, so I'll get them to send the bodies over to you. Just send me the invoice once it's all over."

WITH THAT HE WAS GONE.

Simon worked hard to ensure everything was perfect. He made the old couple look as good as possible for when their daughter Vera came to view them in their open coffins. He felt so sorry for her, she looked absolutely devastated.

"Oh Simon, I can't believe they've gone. It was only a couple of days ago that I saw them and they seemed fine. Now it seems that their gas heater had been faulty for a long time. Why on earth would their landlord not have got it checked out? I thought they were supposed to do safety checks every year? Mum and Dad didn't really like living there you know. Of course they loved being right opposite the beach, Dad always said he could smell the ocean and hear the seagulls the minute he woke up. But I know they missed their old house, the house me and Herbert live in. The house where I was born, where they spent their whole married life. My mum was born there too, I think it rather broke her heart to leave."

"Did they just want to downsize? Perhaps have no stairs? I know my old mum often says she wishes she lived in a bungalow now she's getting older and her knees are playing up a bit."

"Oh no. They'd never talked about moving out until Herbert told them about all the Inheritance Tax I'd have to pay if they left the house to me in their will. He got them really worried. I'm their only child you see and they wanted to make sure I'd always have a roof over my head. And my great grandad built the place, so there were lots of memories there."

She burst into tears and he passed her the box of tissues

that always sat on his desk. He was used to dealing with grieving relatives.

"I wanted us to buy a place of our own, I was looking forward to making a nice home for us, but he said it would be more sensible to buy my mum and dads house and find them a nice little flat on the seafront. Of course he wanted a bargain, beat my dad right down on the price. I was really upset, especially when I realised that it wouldn't leave them enough to buy what they really wanted, one of those nice new retirement flats on the seafront. In a gated community, with a little café and nice neighbours. Herbert said he had a colleague who rented out property, so they ended up doing that instead. I wasn't happy. It was smaller than they wanted, in an old block with a dodgy lift, but it did have nice sea views. I could tell they were unhappy, but Herbert got cross every time I mentioned it. So I just popped in to see them every day when I finished work and they came and had lunch with me at the café in the store where I work every Friday. I feel so guilty that I didn't notice anything about that dodgy heater. I feel like I killed them."

It had taken quite a while for her to calm down. Poor woman. Such a shock to lose your parents unexpectedly like that, and to carry so much guilt.

Of course, the funeral went smoothly. Everything worked like clockwork and Herbert strutted around the place, making sure everyone knew that *he* had organised and paid for the whole affair.

Except that he didn't pay. He never paid, despite Simon sending him invoices, reminders and final demands. In the end, six months later, in desperation, he went into the bank one day and demanded to see Herbert Jones, the manager.

"Oh good day. How are you? Come for another loan have you?"

There was something about the way he said it that made Simon suspicious.

"Oh no, I don't need another loan thank you. The business is doing very well. Sadly we seem to have lost lots of people this winter, the unusually cold spell has been hard for a lot of people. Especially the old pensioners who can't afford to keep their heating on all the time. Actually I've just come about this unpaid bill. I assume none of the others ever reached you, although we did send them to you here at the bank, as you asked. So as not to upset your wife."

"Yes. I did get them, but thought you understood that I expected a hefty discount, as a courtesy. Without me you wouldn't have a share in that business at all. I can't believe you'd have the audacity to send me a bill."

"But Mr. Jones, you demanded the very best of everything. It never occurred to me that you did not intend to pay. They were your in- laws after all. So I understood that you and your wife would want to give them a good send off and we did our very best. We fulfilled our side of the bargain and I must insist that you do too. I will speak to Mr. Bloom and see if we can offer you a generous discount, but we need you to settle the bill in the next week. Otherwise we may have to consider taking legal action."

Jimmy the bank messenger was standing outside the managers door when Simon finally came out. He took the shaking man to the front door and followed him outside.

"Are you okay sir? I heard all the shouting. I'm used to that, he's a difficult man at the best of times."

Herbert Henry Jones, respectable bank manager, never did pay that outstanding invoice. He had become a powerful man in the town and somehow word got back to Simon and Mr. Bloom that if they pursued him for the money, their business reputation might suffer. It was not an idle threat.

Other people in the town had been ruined by such gossip and in the funeral business a blemish free reputation was an absolute necessity.

So, when Simon Blow, undertaker of Bloom & Sons, heard that Herbert Jones had fallen and frozen to death in the snow, he was delighted. In his opinion the man had the ending he deserved.

Of course Vera, the widow, asked him to do the funeral. She had been so impressed with all his firm had done when her parents died that she would not think of going elsewhere. Of course she had absolutely no idea that her husband had refused to settle the bill for their funeral. She had just been grateful that all the worry had been taken out of her hands. It had been hard enough losing them. She would have been mortified if she had realised how badly her husband had behaved.

"Please give him a good send off. There will be lots of people there, important people I expect, so I don't want them to think I'm not giving him the funeral he deserves."

Simon was a consummate professional, so no-one would ever have known his thoughts as he escorted Herbert's coffin into the church and then to the graveyard. He had his sad undertakers face on, but inside he was thrilled to be getting rid of the man who had caused so much misery to so many people.

18

CHARLOTTE

Charlotte Collins was 37 years old. Almost past her prime some might say, but still very attractive. She was one of those people you would describe as beautiful inside and out.

Her life had been rather wonderful until she was 25 and decided to open a teashop. She had always loved baking and everyone said she should do it professionally, but her parents had insisted she got a *proper* job. So she took a secretarial course at the local technical college, passed with flying colours and took a job at the local branch of a nationwide insurance company. At first she was content enough, the work was easy for a smart girl like her and she made lots of new friends there. Whenever it was anybody's birthday she would bake cupcakes for everyone in the office and at Christmas she always produced a huge fruit cake, covered in marzipan and white icing. One year she decorated it to look like a proper snow scene, with little Christmas trees, baubles, handmade holly leaves, berries and even a small Father Christmas figurine. When anyone got married she would offer to make their wedding cake for free, if they paid for the ingredients. After five years of this she heard the comments almost weekly:

"Oh Lottie (hardly anyone called her Charlotte anymore, except for her mum and dad) you really should set up your own business, you're wasted here just typing insurance claims all the time."

Occasionally she allowed herself to dream. How wonderful would it be to be her own boss? Perhaps she could run it from home, start small?

"Oh don't be ridiculous darling. This kitchen isn't at all suitable, I'm pretty sure you need to have a proper commercial kitchen, you know one checked by the local council and all that. It would cost a fortune to convert this one. Just carry on doing your day job, it's a good regular income and you can still make cakes every now and then."

Her mothers word was law. The subject was closed and Lottie gave up on her dreams.

Until her Great Auntie Maud died, leaving her a small inheritance.

"Mum, I think I want to use that money to start a little teashop."

"Oh Charlotte, don't be so ridiculous. You don't know the first thing about running a business. It's not all cream teas and jam sponges you know. There's stuff like tax, rent and hygiene standards. And anyway, that money Aunty Maud left you won't be enough to take on something like that. I think you should just keep it in a savings account for later on, for when you want to get married and buy a house or have kids perhaps. Children are very expensive, you'll be glad of a little nest egg then."

.   .   .

LOTTIE HAD no intention of getting married or having children in the foreseeable future, but she did want to get out of the insurance office. *She* didn't want to be one of those women who stayed there for twenty years or more, watching her life slide away, with no excitement or adventure. Of course she wanted a husband and babies one day, but first she wanted to achieve something for herself, not just making more money for an international conglomerate.

She was wandering around the town one Saturday afternoon a few months later, when she spotted the "For Sale" sign on the old ironmongers shop. It had closed down a few weeks earlier, the old couple who had run it for more than 30 years had finally admitted defeat, they could no longer compete with the huge out of town hypermarkets. Enormous, rather soulless places that sold not just nuts and bolts, saws and drills, but also garden furniture, lighting and garden equipment. They had been very sad to part with their little shop, but could now retire and take life a bit easier.

"Of course Miss, taking on a property like this is not easy you know. Although it's in good shape now, in time you might have to do a bit of maintenance on it. And the rates and insurance bills are quite hefty.

If I'm being honest, the high street is dying a bit, lots of really good businesses have had to pack up, so there's not a lot of foot traffic."

The real estate agent spoke kindly, but wanted to put her off. He had a daughter of a similar age and there was no way she would be able to run a business, even if she had his support behind her.

"Oh I'm not worried about foot traffic. Once they've tasted my cakes they'll definitely come back for more."

She sounded so certain that he laughed.

"Oh Miss, it's not about how good your cakes are. I'm sure they're delicious. But taking on a premises like this is not a piece of cake, if you'll pardon the pun. I think you should think very carefully before you commit yourself to such a venture. It may be 1976 and I know you young ladies think you can take on the world with all this Women's Liberation stuff, but one day you'll all come to your senses and realise that your place is at the kitchen sink, looking after your husband and babies. My girl reckons she can do better than her nice little office job too, but I've persuaded her to stick with it till she gets married. She's almost exactly the same age as you. Ruth her name is."

OF COURSE LOTTIE had no intention of listening to any such sensible advice. In her head she already owned the freehold of the little shop. It was absolutely perfect for her plans. There was just one small hiccup, the money she had got from Great Aunt Maude wasn't quite enough to buy the place outright and she knew that her parents, even if they had a few thousand pounds lying around, would not want to lend it to her for such a risky venture.

"WELL MY DEAR, please take a seat. I understand that you are looking for a loan?"

She had felt rather uncomfortable the minute she walked into his huge wood panelled office. He was charming, a little smarmy to her mind and she hated the way he was looking her body up and down, lingering rather too long on her breasts. She had dressed sensibly for the occasion, wearing her best dress: a blue chiffon one with a high frilly neck, long sleeves and covered most of her legs. But that didn't seem to deter his wandering eyes. She really wished he had allowed his secretary to stay in the room with them, but he had shooed her away.

"Now Miss C .....or perhaps I should call you Charlotte? Tell me exactly what I can do for you?"

She left his office twenty minutes later, flushed and uncomfortable, but at least he had agreed to give her a loan, the exact amount she need to sign the contract and buy the little shop.

It PROVED to be a great success. The opening day was wonderful, her friends from the insurance company and all her old school friends turned up. There was barely standing room. She had decorated (with the help of her dad and uncle) the place beautifully and it was warm and inviting. Each table was covered with a pristine white cloth and fresh flowers in pretty cut glass vases decorated each table. Her cakes stood proudly in the shop window, piled high on old fashioned glass stands. She was completely sold out by 3 o'clock on the first day and although her family were convinced it was *"just a flash in the pan, beginners luck,"* even they had to admit they were wrong, when six weeks later the place was still crowded out every day. Lottie had been right, she could make a success of this!

One afternoon, just as she was about to close up, he walked in. She recognised him immediately.

"Oh hello Mr. Jones. How nice of you to pop in. What do you think of the place. Of course I haven't got any cakes left to offer you, they've all sold out. I'm just going upstairs to make a fresh batch for tomorrow."

"Well my dear, I just had to come. I've been watching you, I

mean your shop, every day when I stroll past on my way to the newsagents to pick up my paper. And of course I've seen all the payments you've made into your account. At this rate you'll pay back that loan in no time. Now, do you think I could see the rest of the place, see what you've done with my money?"

She held her tongue. If only she could answer him back, remind him that it was the bank's money she'd borrowed, not his. But she knew she had been lucky to get the loan in the first place. Lots of banks still wouldn't lend to women unless their husbands or fathers stood as guarantors.

She didn't really want to take him upstairs. That was her own private space, a space she had turned into a home as well as a commercial kitchen. It wasn't big, but she had a tiny lounge and a bedroom big enough for her old single bed, the bed she had slept in since she was three years old. The only bathroom in the whole building was downstairs, so she shared the toilet with her customers, but had a little shower room alongside it that was private.

"So this is where you live as well as work?"

She remembered how uncomfortable he had made her feel when she went into the bank to ask for a loan. She had hated the way he stared at her body. Now it was even worse. She was completely alone with him, upstairs in the apartment that doubled up as her kitchen, lounge and bedroom. She was uncomfortably aware of her unmade bed in the corner, she had been in a rush that morning and had forgotten to straighten the duvet or plump up the cushions that sat on it.

"I think you owe me something for helping you to buy this place. Without my generosity you would still be working in that boring old office. How do you intend to show your gratitude?"

It happened so quickly that she didn't have time to push

him away or scream for help. That probably wouldn't have done much good anyway. He was far stronger than her and very determined to get his own way.

Afterwards he simply left her lying on her bed, sobbing and shocked.

"Well done my dear. That wasn't too bad was it? I think you quite enjoyed it really. Perhaps we'll have to do it another time. Don't bother to get up, I'll let myself out. And I'll lock the door behind me, you don't want anyone unsavoury just walking unannounced into your little shop do you?"

IT TOOK her weeks to get over the shock and foolishly she didn't tell anyone. After all, who would believe her, he was a respectable bank manager after all. But she put a brave face on it, baking every evening and opening her tea shop every morning. A few customers noticed that she was looking a bit peaky, but put it down to her working too hard. She often saw him, walking past and peering in the window, but he never came in and for that she was very grateful. She was just not sure how she could face him.

It was a few months later when she realised she was pregnant. Her heart sank. Of course it was *his* baby, she had been so busy for the last year, planning and opening her shop, that she hadn't dated anyone. At first she tried to ignore it, to pretend that it wasn't happening, but once she couldn't do up her favourite jeans anymore she had to face reality. She told her parents, but never divulged the fathers name. She pretended it was the result of a one night stand (which in a disturbing way it was) with a stranger. Everyone was shocked, they all knew what a sensible, well behaved girl she was, not someone who slept around. Perhaps she had just had too much to drink one night and lost all control?

Her family and friends rallied round and helped and protected her for the rest of her pregnancy. They took turns in running the shop while she attended hospital appointments and when little Grace arrived, her beautiful, healthy baby girl, they were both fussed over. People delivered flowers, cakes and casseroles, and her mum moved in to help her for the first few weeks.

Both Lottie and baby Grace thrived. It turned out that despite everything, she was a marvellous mother and her baby girl became the focus of her world. All the customers in the teashop fussed over her and when she was big enough she loved to help, wearing a little apron that matched her mothers, taking peoples orders and generally charming everyone. She was an absolute delight.

Occasionally Herbert Jones popped into the teashop, on the excuse of buying a few cakes to celebrate someone's birthday. Although usually he sent Jimmy the bank messenger over. She liked Jimmy, he was always so kind and chatty. She always avoided Herbert, making sure that one of the other waitresses served the obnoxious man.

She never told him that Grace was his daughter. He didn't deserve to know. She was just grateful that the little girl looked like her and didn't seem to have inherited any of his features.

She had been shocked when Vera Jones, his wife, had called into the shop shortly after baby Grace was born. She hardly knew the woman, so was surprised when she turned up with a huge bunch of flowers and some pretty baby clothes.

"Oh my dear, she is so beautiful, you must be so thrilled. I

do hope you like the clothes. If they don't fit, just bring them into the shop and we can exchange them for something else. I am a little envious of your beautiful little girl, I lost a few babies myself and am too old to have anymore now. Do enjoy her my dear. It will be hard at first, especially managing on your own and running this place, but I am sure you will do very well."

She cried after the older woman left. How cruel life could be. That lovely lady was obviously so sad about not having children. What on earth would she think if she realised that her own husband had fathered Lottie's baby?

Grace was seven years old when he died. The man who had raped her and fathered her beloved daughter had frozen to death.

She cried at the funeral. Not for him, but for herself and her little girl who would never know the identity of her father. She also cried for Vera his widow. But for the man himself she shed no tears. She was glad he was dead.

Vera Jones always suspected that little Grace was her husband's child. Of course she never mentioned it to anyone, but from the moment she stepped into the tea room and peered into the baby's pram it had been obvious to her. There was just something about the little one, she looked just like her mother, but there was something familiar about the child's eyes, those dark eyes that seemed to stare deep down into your soul.

It had been such a shock. The only reason she had gone to visit them at all was because the baby's grandmother, Lottie's mum, had gone into the department store to buy a pram. She had then popped up to the gloves and scarf department, Vera's domain, to buy a pretty scarf to cheer herself up.

"Oh I think I like this pink one best. And it is a little girl after all."

With that she had burst into tears and poured out the whole sad story to Vera.

"My girls gone and got herself in the family way. She's not married and won't tell us who the father is. My husband looks at every young man like he wants to kill them for ruining our girls life. Anyway, the baby's here now. Beautiful little thing she is and our Charlotte is calling her Grace. She reckons she can still carry on running her teashop, even with a baby in tow. I was hoping she'd give that up and come home, but my girl is stubborn. She says she's going to prove everyone wrong and make a success of her life. I just hope people aren't too unkind to her, you know how people feel about unmarried mothers, even in this day and age."

Vera had listened sadly. She was a little envious of anyone who managed to produce a baby, even if they weren't married. If only *her* babies hadn't died, she would have so loved being a mother.

So one day, a couple of weeks after the baby's birth, she used her staff discount to buy a few little outfits and wrapped them carefully in pink tissue paper. In the teashop she handed the bag to Lottie, who smiled gratefully.

"Would you like to hold her? She's just been fed so she should be quite happy."

VERA WENT HOME and cried buckets of tears. She just knew that her instincts were right, she knew that that dear little baby girl was his. She wondered if he knew? It did seem that Lottie was quite determined to bring the little girl up on her own, so perhaps he wasn't interested. She wondered if it had just been a fleeting affair? Surely that pretty young woman would not want to make a life with a man old enough to be her father, even if he was as charming as she knew her Herbert could be.

She never questioned him, it just never seemed to be the right time.

But she found herself popping into the teashop once a week, always with the excuse of buying a few nice cakes for the women she worked with. But in reality she wanted to see the baby, to watch it grow, to see if it ended up looking like Herbert.

Lottie was always on edge when Vera walked in. Of course, she had never told anyone who the father was, but somehow she sensed that Vera knew. They never discussed it. It was always something that hung in the air between them.

"Shall we go out for tea next Saturday Vera? We could treat ourselves for once. I really like that little tea room on the High Street, they do delicious cakes. Shall we go there? My treat?"

Vera took a while to reply.

"Oh that sounds lovely Betty. It would be a nice treat, I hardly ever go out these days, I guess I just got so used to staying at home at weekends in case Herbert needed me. But now I don't have to worry about that, do I? Not now he's gone. I can't believe it's six months since he died. It'll be Christmas before we know it."

Lottie greeted them like old friends.

"Oh hello you two. So nice to see you both. I really love it

when the summer seasons over and I just get all the locals coming in here. It makes it more homely somehow and of course everyone fusses over my little Grace. Can you believe she's seven now, growing up so fast. She's a real help in the shop these days, she loves helping. Mind you, If she had her way all the cakes would be chocolate with bright pink icing!"

Vera looked across to the counter, where the little girl was perched on a stool. She was deep in conversation with an old man, telling him that next time he ordered a hot chocolate he should ask her mum for extra chocolate sprinkles.

Vera felt her heart thumping in her chest. Yes, she was absolutely certain that Grace was Herbert's child: there was something so familiar about her.

"I was just saying Vera, how well you're doing. That you're a fabulous example of a modern widow. Working full time and running a house singlehandedly."

Vera winced. She really hated any reference to her dead husband, it brought up so many conflicting emotions. She excused herself and went to the bathroom. Sitting on the pink painted stool next to the toilet seat, she shed a few tears.

"Oh dear, I think I've upset her by talking about him. Mind you, I've been hearing a few things lately that make me wonder if he was as good a husband as she thinks he was. There's lots of rumours flying around the town. About how many people he's upset over the years."

Lottie really didn't want to have this conversation. She had never told anybody who fathered her daughter and certainly had no intention of letting his grieving widow find out now.

"Yes, I've heard plenty of stories. Apparently he wasn't quite as nice as we all thought. They say his car, you know that posh

Jaguar he had, was often parked outside the Tiger Inn at East Dean. Everyone knows that's where men take their fancy bits when they want a quiet drink."

"Oh dear, that's really sad for Vera, if it's true. She's such a lovely lady. She was really kind to me after Grace was born, even bought me a few nice baby clothes from that posh department store she works at. They were so lovely that I kept them and now Grace uses them to dress her dollies in."

Lottie knew she was waffling and was glad when Betty spoke again.

"Well, I reckon and I've got it on very good authority." She wasn't going to tell anyone that Andy, the young policeman, had confided his suspicions to her. He might lose his job if she did that.

"I've been told that it might not have been an accident after all. It might have been murder."

"Oh how awful."

Even as she said the words Lottie realised what a hypocrite she was being. How wonderful it would have felt to kill him herself: that dreadful man had ruined her life.

"Well, my source tells me that although it was written off as an accident, some people still believe it wasn't just misadventure. They reckon there are plenty of people who had good reason to see Herbert Jones dead."

At that moment Vera came out of the bathroom and walked back towards them. It was obvious she had been crying.

"Now, what can I get you ladies. We have some lovely coffee and walnut cake today, or some nice cream slices. What do you fancy?"

19

THE SNOOKER CLUB

One of Herbert's passions, apart from power, other women, and his Jaguar car, was snooker. He had been playing the game since he was a teenager. When he was younger he had hung around smokey clubs and pubs, desperate to act like the big man, smoking cigarette after cigarette and flashing his snooker cue around. He became well known in his hometown for being pretty good at it, usually winning every game he played.

By the time he became a bank manager, he had progressed to the more refined atmosphere of the local Conservative Club. It had been easy to get put forward for membership to that rather stuffy institution, lots of people wanted to curry favour with the man who might be able to help them out in future with a bank loan or overdraft.

The "Con" club, as it was known by its members, was housed in a rather splendid building next to the Town Hall. A grand brick built edifice, in a style much loved by the Victorian architects who had flooded to the seaside town in the late 1800's and had left their mark by erecting so many splendid buildings. Red brick buildings with pillars, arches and lots of fancy plasterwork.

Herbert loved the Conservative Club. It suited him absolutely. It was rather stuffy and exclusive, *"They don't let just any old riffraff in"* he was delighted to report to Vera, *"Only the most elite gentlemen in the town can become members."* Of course no ladies were allowed to join. It may have been the 1970's but there were still standards that had to apply.

"Delicate creatures like you my dear, are of course welcomed for special events, fundraisers and the like, even the Christmas party, but it is a gentleman's haven, somewhere we can relax and discuss business and the state of the world, quietly over a glass or two of whisky. Not a suitable place for women at all. Although there are a few younger members who are pushing for change. I think their wives are behind it all. Next they'll be expecting to be allowed in the snooker rooms, Damn ridiculous. These young chaps should learn to keep their wives in order."

He loved the atmosphere of the place. The way everyone knew his name and treated him with deference. The way all the drinks were subsidised. The way everyone dressed decently, either in a full business suit or just a smart jacket, tie and well pressed trousers. You would never see a crumpled shirt at the Con Club. The members all had wives or mothers at home to ensure they always looked their best.

Herbert had no idea that so many other members despised him. Of course they were polite to his face, they were all gentlemen of course. But behind his back they gossiped. They were all local men; some ran businesses; some were shopkeepers; a few were landed gentry; and some were just ordinary working men. But they tried to behave well, never swearing or being rude in front of women.

They had all heard the rumours, and seen the results of Herbert's unpleasant arrogance.

They had seen him make the young barmaid at the club cry, when she accidentally poured him the wrong brand of whiskey: a cheap blend instead of the twelve year old malt he had ordered. They had been horrified as he loudly berated her and one brave soul, the club chairman, had stepped in and led Herbert gently away, reminding him *"Come on old chap, no need to carry on like that, the lass just made a mistake. She's new, probably just a bit nervous having to deal with all us fine gents."*

He upset lots of the other club members by constantly reminding them of his power. They knew that if they upset him he would be unlikely to grant them a business loan or overdraft and so many of them kowtowed to him, pretending a friendship that didn't really exist. A few times they had caught him cheating, moving the snooker balls when he thought no-one was looking. Of course he behaved well during proper club matches: there was no way he wanted to be found out, to be outed as a scoundrel, a man who behaved badly.

Simon Billings, another member at the club, often behaved badly. He was not a loyal husband, but he treated his children and his mother very well. His wife, to whom he had been married for more than 30 years was used to his wandering ways, he had done it for almost all of their married life. For the first two years he was a loyal loving husband, but once the babies came along he felt pushed out and sought solace in the arms of his secretary. That young woman was thrilled, she had lusted after him for a long time, after all he was good-looking, charming and rich, and she fell for his charms. He persuaded her that he was going to leave his wife, buy them a little house in the country and live happily ever after, but when his babies started to grow and turn into interesting little people, he knew he could never leave them.

Now they were grown up, living their own lives and he saw them only occasionally, mostly when they needed to borrow some money or use his contacts. But he didn't care. He loved them deeply. He also loved his mother deeply. She had brought him up single-handedly, after his father had shot himself in the head following a failed business venture. Simon had only been 10 years old at the time but he remembered it very clearly. He had loved and looked up to his father and knew that his suicide still affected him greatly. Not that it was really any excuse for all his bad behaviour over the years. So many different women. But at least that had been his only vice. And his wife understood, so much so that they were now good friends, still sharing the same great big house, still eating at the same table, still going together to all the Masonic balls, still sleeping together occasionally: usually after too many glasses of champagne. He still had lovers, but she did too these days. And it seemed to work for them both.

But despite his own failings, he loathed and detested the way Herbert Jones operated.

In his opinion, that man was not a gentleman. He treated people very badly, spoke down to them and was arrogant and rude. There were always plenty of rumours flying around the club about his behaviour, it was hard to keep secrets in a small town. Simon had, on many occasions, spotted Herbert's distinctive Jaguar car in remote spots: the car parks at Birling Gap and Beachy Head, or tucked into a quiet layby at the foot of the South Downs. He knew all the signs of course, He had often used those venues for his own liaisons. But the thing he hated most about the man was the way he treated the lovely Vera, his wife. He knew that was rather ironic, considering he was a wayward husband himself, but at least he was always respectful in public. Herbert on the other hand behaved abominably at times. He would talk down to Vera, criticising her in front of other people, belittling her words, acting as though she was somehow beneath him, not worthy of being a bank managers wife. Simon often wondered how Vera put up with him, she must be a saint.

VERA DIDN'T MIND Herbert going to the snooker club. She quite looked forward to her Tuesday, Friday and sometimes Saturday nights off. He would go there straight from work, so she didn't even have to bother to cook on those days. Instead she could indulge in one of her favourites: Welsh Rarebit or Scrambled Eggs on Toast. They both reminded her of her childhood, all those happy times growing up in this house, with her lovely mum and dad. As she stood in the kitchen, stirring the eggs in the saucepan, she remembered her mum doing exactly the same. On Sunday nights mostly. The one day of the week when they all relaxed and sat with their dinner on their laps watching Sunday Night at the London Palladium on the television. Such happy times.

Of course Herbert would not approve of such behaviour. They had done it a few times in the early days, when her mum and dad still lived in the house with them, but she had known, by his body language, that he hated behaving in such a casual manner. So now that her parents were both dead, she had to lay the table every day, with a fresh tablecloth and linen napkins. Woe betide her if she got sloppy and put a jar of jam or marmalade, or bottle of sauce, on the table. He would glare at her and ask why she hadn't decanted them into nice cut glass dishes. It was no wonder that she looked forward to her nights off. She really wouldn't have minded if he went to the snooker club every night. In fact sometimes she wondered how she would feel if he wasn't there at all. Everything had seemed so much simpler before he came into her life. Now all she seemed to do was walk on eggshells every day, doing her absolute best to make him happy. She had come to realise over the years, that an unhappy Herbert was not easy to handle. Far better to squash her own hopes and dreams to ensure he was content. Of course, in the old days, when her mum and dad were still alive, she could talk to them about it. She was always careful how much she said though. The last thing she wanted was for her dad to confront him, that would just make matters worse. Of course she knew they had never approved, that they didn't really like her husband. But they, like her, seemed determined to just make the best of a bad situation. They certainly never encouraged her to leave him or think about divorce. She never knew exactly how Herbert had forced them to move out of their own house, selling it to him at below the market price. Or why they agreed to move into that horrid little flat on the seafront, in the rather tatty building owned by a friend of his, instead of the lovely brand new, purpose built retirement apartment she had found for them. Her dad had been cagey when she asked, fobbing her off with some flimsy explanation about body corp fees and building maintenance costs. Although she was worried, she hadn't questioned him too much, he was her dad after all and she had always looked up to him. She had really hoped they were making the right decision.

It had felt strange living in her childhood home, knowing her parents were just down the road in a rather gloomy small flat. She had tried standing up to Herbert, telling him she would much rather her parents stayed in their own house until they died and that she really didn't care if she inherited less because of this. But he was adamant. And when Herbert Jones was adamant it was almost impossible to change his mind.

For the first few months, her parents came to the house every Sunday for a nice roast dinner. Vera loved having them there. She would lay the table with the best china (inherited from her grandma) and use the lovely crystal wine glasses her aunty had given her as a wedding present. Her mum would be in the kitchen helping to prepare the roast dinner, as they had done together almost every Sunday for the last 30 years. Her dad would sit in the lounge, listening patiently as Herbert droned on about whatever subject was important to him that week. Sometimes it was cars, sometimes the state of the world. But whatever it was, the conversation was always one sided, her dad was rarely allowed to get a word in. Instead he would sit there quietly fuming. *"How on earth does my precious girl put up with this insufferable arrogant bloke?"* Sometimes he wished Herbert would just drop dead mid-sentence. Then at least his girl would be free. He knew, just knew, that she wasn't truly happy in her marriage, however brave a face she put on it.

20

TONY

Tony hadn't done very well at school. Mostly because he didn't bother to concentrate. He didn't see what good learning about algebra, fractions, the Kings of England and the War of the Roses was going to do for his future. All he wanted to do was be a chef and own the best restaurant in town. Surely that wasn't too much to ask for?

Of course, because he was so busy dreaming, he got left behind. He failed all his exams and ended up being disruptive in class. And then he got caught up with a bad crowd, older boys who only cared about drinking, smoking and having a good time. Unfortunately their idea of a good time was stealing cars and breaking into peoples houses.

Luckily Tony still had a bit of common sense and he gradually left their little gang. He didn't want to end up in trouble with the law, or even go to prison. No, he just wanted to be a chef.

Being a poor boy from a rather rough council estate didn't open up too many opportunities for him. He didn't have a wealthy father to bankroll him, or good family contacts to find him work in a fine establishment. Instead he had an absent father, gone since he was just 3 years old, leaving Tony, his mum and his baby sister to cope with life alone. His mum did her best, cleaning houses for rich people in the daytime then working at the bingo hall four nights a week.

So, when Tony left school at the age of 16 his only options were the local fishing industry; but he hated the sea and didn't like killing things; or to become a builders labourer, lugging heavy bags of cement and bricks around all day long. It was hard work, but he was a fit young man. In time he came to quite enjoy the job, it wasn't taxing on his brain and he gained muscles from all the heavy lifting. He was a good looking chap, six feet tall, dark haired with twinkly brown eyes and the girls loved him. He was polite, charming and respectful, a real gentleman.

One day, just after his 23rd birthday, he decided it was time to pursue his dream. He was more realistic these days and knew that he was unlikely to become a top chef, there were too many of those already for him to compete, but he was determined to better himself. So, he signed up to a catering course at the local polytechnic college. It was just a two year course, but if he stuck it out, he would end up with a catering certificate.

The two years passed quickly and he loved every moment. Sometimes he wished he had done it earlier, gone there straight from school, but of course he hadn't been in a fit state to do such a thing then. He had been far too busy experimenting with drink, drugs and girls. It had taken a few years to sort himself out, the lure of being a bad boy was so strong. A lot of his mates back then had got into trouble with the police, a few had even ended up going to prison, or become full blown drug addicts. But fortunately, thanks mostly to the constant support of his lovely mum, he had survived and was now thriving. He often shuddered thinking about what could have happened if his mum hadn't kept him on the straight and narrow. He would always be thankful to her. If he had got found in possession of a knife, he doubted he would ever have been allowed to start a catering course, after all there was an abundance of sharp knives in every commercial kitchen.

And he was now a dab hand with a sharp knife, he could cut and fillet almost anything.

For the first few years after graduating, he took on junior roles in the kitchens of basic restaurants. But he always had big dreams. One day he intended to open his own restaurant.

At the time of Herberts death he was working for Maria Finch, owner of La Scala, the most popular Italian restaurant in town. She was a good boss, firm but fair. She had inherited the business from her father and ran it in the same authentic way that the old man had done. The only thing she had changed was the colour of the napkins. He had always loved red and white checked ones, but she preferred plain white ones, they were much easier to launder, using a bit of bleach to remove any stubborn red wine or tomato sauce stains.

He and Maria had become good friends. She often joked that if she was 20 years younger, she would take him as her lover. Some people would have thought that was an inappropriate comment for an employer to make to one of their staff members, but Tony didn't care, he was flattered that such a fabulous woman even gave him a second glance. Although she was in her sixties, Maria could easily have passed for a woman in her 40's. She was slim, with glossy dark hair and had flawless olive toned skin. Her face and figure had retained their youthful glow and she often joked that it was because she had never saddled herself with a husband, unlike her younger sisters, who, while still attractive, now had rather more matronly figures.

Maria and Tony became firm friends very quickly. There was a lot of natural chemistry between them, but this wasn't affected by anything physical, they were just platonic friends. It would have been very easy, after a long shift and too many glasses of red wine, to have ended up in bed together, especially as Maria lived over the restaurant, but they were both very conscious that it might destroy their friendship, a friendship they had each come to value enormously.

"What's wrong Tony love?"

He had been rather quiet for the whole evening, which wasn't like him, he was usually so gregarious.

"Oh nothing really, I'm alright."

"That's rubbish, you're obviously not ok, you didn't even flirt with young Maisie tonight."

He blushed, she was right, he was an awful flirt and Maisie the new waitress was awfully pretty. Far too young for him of course.

He cleared his throat, trying to buy time before he spoke.

"Oh Maria. I didn't want to tell you till I was sure, but it doesn't matter now anyway."

"What doesn't matter?"

"Well, you know you're thinking of selling that little shop opposite the pier?"

"Do you mean the old ice cream parlour?"

"*Yes. You were saying the other day that you don't need it now you've opening the big one on the High Street. So I'd been thinking I might see if you'd sell it to me. So I could open a place of my own. You know that's always been my dream.*"

"*But it's a bit small for a restaurant love.*"

"*Oh I know I couldn't do sit down meals, but I thought it could be a take away burger bar. Tony's Burgers.*"

She looked like she was going to cry. Tough old Maria Finch. He was horrified that he'd upset her.

"*But don't worry love, that dream's not going to happen. I went to the bank today to try and get a loan. Thought I'd sort it all out, then present you with my proposal. But I can't now. That bastard wouldn't lend me the money. Said I was just a cook, with no assets and no prospects. Said I was a very bad risk and certainly not the kind of person his bank would lend money to.*"

He sounded close to tears, so Maria walked over and put her arm around him.

"*Oh love. I'm sorry. What bank did you go to, perhaps you could try another one.*"

"*I saw that Mr. Jones, manager of the branch in the High Street, opposite the Leg of Mutton pub. He was really rude and arrogant, spoke down to me the whole time. Acted like I was just dirt on his shoes. It didn't seem to impress him that I've been saving money out of my wages every week and now have a tidy little sum in my account. He told me that I should just be grateful to have a job here. He said he knew that you treated your staff fairly. In fact, he seemed to sing your praises. Maybe he fancies you. I couldn't blame him for that.*"

Maria went very quiet. It took her several minutes to reply and when she did, her voice was ice cold.

"*Tony, do not take any notice of what that man says. He is a disgusting, unpleasant creature, the kind of man who should have been castrated at birth."*

He had never heard her speak like that before. Not his gorgeous Maria. She was always so calm and controlled, so kind to everybody.

"I am going to tell you something now Tony, but you must promise me it never passes your lips. It must remain our secret. Can you promise me this?"

He nodded, unsure of what she was going to say. Of course he would keep her secret. He would love this woman, even though she was nearly thirty years his senior, until the day he died. There was no-one else in the whole world that he desired so much.

They sat in the darkened restaurant until two in the morning. He was horrified as she told him the sad story of her little sister Rosa, the girl who had, at the age of 19, found herself pregnant and abandoned. How Rosa, unable to cope with the shame she had brought on her Catholic family, had taken her own life a few years later. He was shocked and disgusted to hear that the father of Rosa's baby was none other than Herbert Jones, now a respectable bank manager, who had that very day, refused him a business loan.

Their shared secret drew them even closer together. Tony gave up his dream of a burger bar, and Maria, appreciating his support and loyalty, signed half of her restaurant over to him, on the understanding that he moved into the flat upstairs with her. They were very discreet, but it was obvious to everyone that they were madly in love. The years ticked by and their hatred for Herbert grew. They often fantasised, over a bottle of wine, of the horrific things they would do to him.

They often bumped into him, in the street or at local

Business Association functions, but he had no idea of the dark thoughts going through their heads.

They attended his funeral together, holding hands throughout the church service and later at the graveyard, delighted that the man who had ruined so many lives had finally got his just deserts. Frozen to death. Alone. They hoped he had suffered.

21

**TERRANCE (CHAIRMAN OF THE
BUSINESS ASSOCIATION)**

Terrance Thomas was an ordinary boy who had made good. Born into a big family, living on a rather rough council estate in the poorest part of town, he had learnt early how to stand up for himself. At first it was his brothers and sisters he had to contend with, all seven of them fighting constantly for their mothers attention, the last roast potato or slice of toast. He realised that if he was going to succeed in life he had to be tough, not just physically, but emotionally too. That way he was sure he would be able to cope with whatever life threw at him.

He soon became known just as TT and that became his badge of honour. His siblings had sensible Irish names like Patrick, Paul, Martha, Joan, Mary and Kathleen, but by the time he, the youngest, was born, his mum had tired of giving her babies sensible names, so she called him after her favourite actor: Terence Stamp. Unfortunately, when his dad went to register the baby's birth, he did so after sinking a few pints at the pub (*just to wet the baby's head you know*) and inadvertently spelt the name wrong on the legal document. So instead of being registered as Terence Stamp Thomas as his mother intended, he became Terrance Thomas. She was furious and never quite forgave her husband for this error, but by the time he was three, everyone called him TT.

He was smarter than his brothers and sisters, none of them excelled at school and their ambitions were different to his. They wanted to become builders, hairdressers or shorthand typists, but TT had bigger dreams.

He left school at 16, as most ordinary kids did in the 1960's. Going on to further education, college or university was never an option for him. But he soon realised, after working as a junior clerk in a big insurance company, that he was capable of more. He found the work easy, breezed through every day and by 3 o'clock in the afternoon had finished all his jobs and would wander around the office asking if he could help any of his colleagues. He was soon noticed by the senior management and offered promotion. By the time he was 21 he was running a whole department: a small one of course, but a big responsibility nevertheless and one that paid him well. He became known as a solid, likeable, and hard- working man, appreciated by his colleagues and bosses alike. After 20 years of working there, barely ever taking a day's sick leave, he was appointed to one of the branch manager positions and asked if he would like to join the local Business Association as a company representative.

"Oh Beryl, I do feel a bit out of my depth there, some of those blokes are so rich and important."

"Don't be ridiculous love. You're just as good as them. Look how far you've come. Me and the kids are so proud of you."

He leant across the dinner table and took her hand.

Their three children groaned at the sight of such open affection. Their mum and dad could be so soppy at times.

"Oh love, thank you."

He beamed at his family sitting around the table. How he loved each and every one of them.

Marrying his Beryl was the best thing he had ever done. He had met her at work, when he was just 19 years old and they had quickly become inseparable. In those days, office romances were frowned upon, one partner often got transferred to another branch, but because he was such a good worker, his bosses turned a blind eye. They were married two years later and Beryl gave up work as soon as their first baby was born. Now, the kids were all teenagers, but she was still a stay at home mum, by choice. She didn't want them to be latch key kids and anyway TT earned a very good salary. Enough to have bought their little semi-detached house in a nice leafy street near the beach, to drive a smart car and have nice family holidays every year. She and the kids wanted for nothing, he saw to that. So, all in all he loved his life. He loved his wife, his kids, their house and living by the seaside, the same seaside where his parents and siblings still lived. Most of them had stayed on the rough council estate where they had grown up and they often teased him about being a snob and having a posh house and a posh job. But in reality they were all very proud of him, proud of how hard he had worked to become the successful man he was.

The only fly in TT's world was Herbert Jones. That loud, arrogant and unpleasant man had become the bane of TT's life. They were both members of the local Business Association and as ordinary members their paths had rarely crossed. TT always tried to avoid the bank manager. He had once tried to get a car loan and been turned down. Admittedly he had only been young then, newly married with a big mortgage, but he still remembered how humiliated he had been by Herbert's refusal.

"Now I don't think you're thinking this through properly old chap. You're very young and I know you have a fairly decent job, but you've only got one wage coming now your wife's pregnant and I daresay she'll want to pop out a few more babies, so it would be very unwise for me to loan you any money. I suggest you keep driving that old heap for a few years, then pop back and ask me again when your finances are in better order."

TT could still remember how his cheeks had burnt with embarrassment and anger. His hatred of Herbert had started at that point and he had transferred his account to another bank the following week. There was no way he was ever going to give that dreadful man the satisfaction of talking down to him again.

Of course he saw him often around town, in a small place like Eastbourne it was impossible to avoid someone indefinitely, but they never exchanged a word. Until TT was voted in as Chairman of the Local Business Association.

He was very well liked and had been a great addition to the association, serving his time as both committee secretary and treasurer, so was an obvious choice. But Herbert was jealous, both of his position (one he had always hankered after himself) and his popularity with the other men. He started making snide remarks during public meetings, trying to belittle TT.

"I say, I know our chairman has strong opinions, but does his background really qualify him? I understand his brothers run a building company, but I think we should look further afield, get a decent firm in, not just some backstreet, fly-by-night lads. I could recommend some decent people."

TT's best friend and the associations co-chairman Phil, held up his hand.

"Now, now Mr. Jones. I don't think we should be talking like that. TT's brothers firm has done some jolly good work for this town. They are local, reliable and much fairer on their prices than some of the bigger fancy companies. I vote we stick with them. Let's put it to the vote."

Of course, TT's brothers got the job, they had proved themselves time and time again and were the obvious choice. TT had been very open about the family connection and always refrained from voting if his brothers were one of the suggested contractors.

Herbert Jones hated being thwarted. It became his habit to question TT at every opportunity, trying to put his integrity into doubt. But fortunately most of the other men in the association took no notice of his vitriol, many of them had also had unpleasant dealings with the arrogant bank manager.

So, when they read in the local newspaper, the obituary of Herbert Henry Jones, Bank Manager, fine upstanding member of the community and devoted husband to Vera, there were no tears. The man who had been so unpleasant, had spoilt so many meetings, would do so no longer. They were free of him.

22

PHIL (TRAVEL AGENT)

Phil, TT's best friend and co-chairman on the Business Association committee was a travel agent.

Phil had always wanted to be a travel agent. His dad had been a travel agent and his granddad, now aged 92, had set up the original business back in the 1920's when he had bought an old rundown shop in the High Street, next door to an Italian restaurant. He had become good friends with Carlo Bianchi, the restaurant owner and they had spent a few years enjoying all the pleasures that being young, handsome and charming afforded them.

They had both met and married good women and still remained close, becoming godfathers to each other's children. Their families were pretty interwoven, they lived next door to each other, in the flats above their businesses and their children went to school together and played together. There were even a few romances as the years went on and one young couple married, joining the two families together forever. By now, Carlo had changed his name by deed poll to Finch, thinking it would be easier for his family to assimilate into Eastbourne society if they had a more Anglicised name. He kept the Italian names for his restaurants and ice cream parlour, it seemed that the slight exoticness of the Bianchi name made them more enticing to the customers.

His Grandfathers travel agency had thrived. In the late 1920's and 1930's foreign travel was only for the wealthy, and Eastbourne was full of such people. Many of them lived in the grand mansions along the seafront, the Old Town or the exclusive leafy streets of the Meads district. They wanted to explore the world, to try the new commercial aircraft which would whisk them in luxury to places like Paris and Rome, to travel to Venice by rail on the opulent Orient Express train, or to go by ship to Calcutta, or New York.

By the time Phil started work in the business in the late 1960's travel had changed beyond all recognition. It was no longer just for the wealthy elite. The old Imperial Airways had, in 1935, joined forces with Qantas Empire Airways to run the first passenger service from London to Brisbane. The trip, known as the Kangaroo Route, had taken 12 and a half days and only operated weekly. Then in 1938 Imperial Airways had introduced flying boat services from Southampton to Australia. These were dubbed "veritable flying hotels" and could accommodate 24 passengers and five crew.

By 1939 these were flying to Egypt, East and West Africa, South Africa, Malaya, Hong Kong, India and Sydney Australia several times a week. In 1967 BOAC introduced its Pacific route to Australia, via New York, San Francisco, Honolulu and Fiji, the entire trip taking a mere 33 hours.

Phil loved learning all about the history of aviation: what routes were taken, what the interior of the planes were like. Fortunately his grandfather was a mine of information. Not only had he lived through those early days, but he had kept everything: all the old posters and articles. His boxes of stuff were like gold dust to the young Phil.

He insisted on framing lots of the old posters and hanging them on the walls of the shop. Sometimes he made window displays, with artefacts from the destinations. He made a South Seas Island window display, using old posters, tickets and photographs, draped with colourful sarongs and leis. When he did an Indian window, he borrowed beautiful saris and bangles from the little Indian dress shop and put red flowers and saffron robes on the floor of the display. Another time, he borrowed skis, hats and scarves from the sports shop to do a display about Austrian and Italian ski resorts. The shop quickly became known as an interesting knowledgeable place, where you could be sure of getting excellent advice on where you should take your next foreign holiday.

Sometimes, Phil's grandfather, now aged 93, a little unsteady on his feet and rather hard of hearing, would sit in the shop watching Phil as he painstakingly set up his window displays.

"That lad reminds me of myself. I was young and enthusiastic too, wanting to make a name for myself. Old Carlo often used to say I had the gift of the gab and an eye for detail. Mind you, me and him were very alike, two young lads willing to take a chance to prove ourselves. Everyone said we were crazy, but look how it's all turned out. We may be doddery old men now, but we've left a great legacy for our families. None of them are going to have to struggle the way we did."

. . .

BOTH OLD MEN died a few years later, within days of each other. It was almost as though they knew their work on earth was done. They had established good businesses, businesses that still provided both their families with an excellent living. Businesses that could go on for several more generations if they were managed well.

PHIL BECAME A GREAT MANAGER. His dad still worked in the business occasionally, but he had pretty much retired, leaving Phil in sole charge. Sometimes Phil thought he was the happiest man on earth. He had a job he loved, a wife he adored, two adorable children and no money worries. The freehold shop his grandfather had wisely bought back in the 1920's had gone up considerably in value and was now worth close to a million pounds. The only blot on Phil's horizon was Herbert Jones.

In his opinion, Herbert Jones was a monster: an unpleasant, disloyal and arrogant man. Phil knew for a fact that Herbert cheated on his lovely wife Vera. Vera was a great friend of his wife Sarah. They had met while both working in Bobby's department store when they were in their twenties. Nowadays they didn't see so much of each other, Sarah was busy at home with the children and Vera still worked full time, but once a month they would go to the Italian restaurant next door (now run by Carlo's daughter Maria and her boyfriend Tony) followed by a trip to the cinema. He knew how much they both looked forward to their monthly excursions.

He had never warmed to Vera's husband Herbert. He considered him to be ill mannered, arrogant and exceedingly unpleasant. He often wondered how the lovely Vera put up with such a brute. Perhaps he was nicer in private?

Anyway, Phil knew, without a shadow of a doubt, that Herbert was an unfaithful husband. It wasn't just the local gossip that made him think that, but the fact, the indisputable fact, that he had on several occasions been asked to book them a weekend away at a luxury hotel, *"I expect you to get me a good deal old chap, after all you never know when you might need to seek a loan or overdraft. By the way, I insist on the best room, sea views if possible and of course a private bathroom. Champagne and chocolates on arrival."*

At first Phil had been happy to comply, thinking how nice it would be for Vera to have a luxurious weekend away. It would do her no end of good, especially after all the sadness of those miscarriages. His wife had told him about them, tears pouring down her face as she spoke of her friends distress. She had been lucky enough to give birth to three healthy children and it upset her greatly that her dear friend Vera could never know the same joy.

Phil had been shocked to later find out that Vera hadn't gone at all.

"Did Vera enjoy her weekend away love? That husband of hers certainly pulled out all the stops to make sure she had a good time."

Obviously the wretched man had taken another woman away with him.

IT HAPPENED several times over the years. Herbert would call into the travel agency, demanding that Phil stop what he was doing and serve him immediately. He refused to be attended to by any of the other qualified and well trained agents working there. Every time he insisted on booking top of the range hotels, in far flung locations, places you could carry on a quiet tryst without being discovered. And every time Phil realised later, that it was not his wife Vera that he took as his guest. He began to stop telling his wife Sarah about the bookings. She obviously did not want to hurt her friend by telling her that her husband was being unfaithful, and Phil did not want his wife to carry the burden of too much deceit. And so he carried on making the bookings as Herbert demanded. He felt disgusted: with Herbert for being unfaithful and with himself for seemingly condoning such behaviour. But the truth was that he didn't want to attract the bank managers wrath. He had heard, through the town grapevine gossip, of several people who had crossed him in some way and it had never ended well. He had no wish to bring misfortune on his travel business, he knew only too well how idle malicious gossip could destroy people and their livelihood. Just look what had happened to Elsie, that lovely young woman who had opened a beauty parlour.

THE YEARS PASSED and Herbert continued with his dalliances. Sometimes Phil thought about telling Vera himself, but he could not bear to upset her. She was a very private person, and although she popped into the travel agents regularly to pick up more brochures, she never seemed to want to discuss her marriage, even in a casual way. She and Sarah continued with their monthly outings, year after year. In fact they had been together on the very night that Herbert died. As usual they had enjoyed a nice Italian meal at Maria Finch's place, followed by a trip to the cinema. Vera had no idea she would end that day as a widow.

THE SOUTH DOWNS, Beachy Head, Seven Sisters and Birling Gap. All local beauty spots.

When a man wants to cheat on his wife, it is important that he finds places to take his lovers. Places where he is unlikely to be spotted. Not just fancy hotels or discreet restaurants and pubs, but places in the countryside too.

Herbert Jones was something of an expert at this.

Having grown up further along the coast in Newhaven, he knew the area very well. Before moving to the Eastbourne branch of the bank, he had worked for a few years in Seaford, another seaside resort some 13 miles away. So his knowledge of quiet secluded places in the vicinity was great. He also knew of places near Brighton: the South Downs was a haven for lovers, with lots of quiet lanes where you could park a car and indulge in a little love making without being disturbed.

BEACHY HEAD and Birling Gap were favourite haunts of his. At dusk, once the tourists had left, both had quiet car parks where you could either conduct your romance in peace, or leave your car where it would probably go unnoticed and stroll, hand in hand with your lover, to find a quiet corner. Of course you had to be careful not to go too near the edge of the cliffs, both places were notorious suicide spots. Herbert had often wondered how many dissatisfied husbands had toyed with the idea of taking their wives there on the promise of a romantic evening stroll, before pushing them to their deaths. Perhaps that was why Vera never fancied going there for a little outing? Not that *he* would do such a thing of course. She was a decent enough wife, even though he didn't find her that exciting anymore. He much preferred the company of younger women, women who would flatter him, tell him how handsome and what a good lover he was.

No, *he* would never think of doing such an awful thing to his wife. After all, as everyone knew, *he* was a perfect gentleman.

23

ELSIE (BEAUTY PARLOUR OWNER)

Elsie Lovett had grown up in Eastbourne.

Her family had lived there for generations, the Lovett's were a well-known and much respected family in the town. Her father, grandfather and brothers were all fishermen and when they weren't selling the day's catch from their makeshift stall on the beach, they were volunteering at the local lifeboat station. Lovett men had been volunteers for the Royal National Lifeboat Institution (better known as the RNLI) for more than a hundred years. In fact several of them were listed on the Wall of Remembrance, having lost their lives trying to save others. Being a lifeboat man was a dangerous occupation.

Elsie loved all her family, but she had a very close bond with her three brothers. They were all older than her, they had always protected her. They had taught her how to catch fish, how to fillet and cook them. She had grown up loving the ocean. Loving it, but respecting the power of it: after all it had claimed the life of several of her uncles. She was a strong swimmer, but knew never to go too far from shore and always to look out for unexpected rips and large waves.

Her brothers always hoped she would join them in the family fishing business, they had two boats now and really wanted to keep it in the family rather than employing strangers. But as Elsie grew she became more girly. She stopped wearing jeans and grubby old jumpers and instead persuaded their mother to buy her pretty dresses. By the time she was 19 it was obvious to them all that she had big dreams. Dreams that didn't include getting up in the middle of the night to catch the best fish, or stand on the freezing cold beach on winter mornings, gutting and filleting the days catch ready for sale.

She had announced when she left school at 17 that she wanted to do a beauty course instead: to learn all about skincare, manicures and massage. Nothing they said would dissuade her. So she signed up for a two year course at the local technical college and absolutely blossomed. She had found her niche and graduated as top of her class, with distinction.

She then found a job at a beauty salon in Brighton, a very smart establishment which catered for wealthy women with the time and money to indulge themselves. She stayed there for five years, learning everything she possibly could. She became an expert at facials, head massages, manicures and pedicures and loved her job.

One day, the shop owner told her that she was intending to retire, to sell the business and move to a villa in Spain. The lease on the shop was up and the greedy landlord was demanding an enormous increase in the rent.

"I'm sorry love. You've been a great worker, all my clients love you, but I just can't keep going any longer. It's high time I retired

and put my feet up in the sunshine. I was hoping that someone would buy me out and take the business over, but the huge increase in rent is putting them off. It would be really hard to make much of a profit on those figures. But you're a smart girl, I'm sure you'll pick up another job easily enough."

Elsie was sad to leave, but she had a plan. She would find a little shop in Eastbourne and set up her own beauty parlour. She had enough experience now to know how it all worked and had plenty of ideas. It would be nice to work nearer to home, although she had loved the excitement and bustle of Brighton, she had hated the commute there, especially in the depths of winter.

"OK everyone, I have an announcement."

It was a Saturday evening and the whole family was sitting around the big kitchen table. Tonight they were eating delicious fresh cod, served with their mum's crispy chips and a bit of salad.

"I'm going to open my own shop and I've found a place on the seafront that will be perfect."

She waited a moment, allowing that bit of news to sink in.

"And the place will need a bit of work doing, painting and a few shelves and things, so I'm hoping you'll all be able to help me. I want to open in a month's time, so I can catch all the Christmas trade. Then I'll be well established by the time summer comes and all the tourists arrive."

"Oh love, that's really exciting, good for you. I'm so proud of you."

Her mum sounded close to tears.

"Well done love, but how are you going to pay for all this? Will you need to get a bank loan? That might be a bit hard, what with you being young and a girl. Banks still aren't very keen on

lending money to women, unless they've got a husband or father to guarantee it."

Her dad sounded anxious.

"Don't worry Dad. I've saved up quite a lot, enough to cover the rent for the first six months or so and I was hoping you and the boys could supply all the paint and timber, and work for free of course!"

"Well, where exactly is this shop then? We'd better come and take a look at it."

And so, the following day, the whole family went to inspect the premises.

Occupying the bottom half of an old Victorian building opposite the pier, the shop was in an excellent position. There was street parking directly outside and a public car park just around the corner. Elsie realised that this was important, as most of her clients would want to drive there.

"This area gets pretty busy in the summer season you know love. It'll be jolly hard for your clients to find a park sometimes, do you think that'll put them off?'

"Oh no Dad, don't worry, by then I'll have established myself. They'll be so desperate to get an appointment they won't care how far away they have to park. After all, I'll be running the best beauty parlour in town."

"So who exactly is your landlord? Is it someone local, someone we know? Perhaps I could talk to him, get you a bit of a discount?"

"This whole block used to be owned by Carlo Finch. He bought it when he first came here from Italy, back in the 1920's. He was a really nice bloke, my old dad used to go to the pub with him and play Whist.

But I heard that after he died, the family sold a lot of their property, just keeping the restaurants and ice cream parlours. Mind you,

I reckon that means they still own plenty, and of course all those old places have lovely apartments over the shops. I often fancied moving into one of them myself, but your mum wouldn't budge, she loves our house, says it holds too many memories to leave behind."

"Apparently the building is now owned by some company. But the rent is pretty good and once the boys have worked their magic I reckon it's going to look fabulous."

She was right. Just a few weeks later *Elsie's* opened its doors for the first time. Inside everything was pristine. Her father and brothers had done a great job. The walls were painted in a delicate shade of pink, the floor was covered in a pale wood effect vinyl (much more practical for regular mopping than real wood) and the pine shelving held a mixture of green plants and lotions and potions in fancy glass bottles with pink labels. There were sofas and chairs adorned with pretty pink cushions and piles of fluffy pink towels stood by the counter. All in all it was a very pleasant, girly establishment.

ELSIE WORKED HARD for the first few months. She couldn't afford to employ anyone else until the shop started to make a profit, but fortunately she had plenty of friends, girls she had met at college, who were only too happy to lend her a hand at weekends, in exchange for a manicure or facial. It was a very happy working environment. The clients were delighted to have somewhere to go locally, rather than having to drive all the way to Brighton every time they fancied a facial or a manicure. Elsie's place was not just handy, it also provided an excellent service. Her reputation soared and she soon made enough money to start taking a small weekly wage herself, as well as thinking of taking on an assistant full time.

There were a few hiccups of course. The boiler which provided the hot water and serviced the radiators was old and a bit leaky. At first it was just an annoyance, so she sent a polite message to her landlords, asking them if they could fix it. Weeks later, despite her repeated requests, nothing had been done, so her dad said he would call them.

"Sorry love, but they probably aren't taking you very seriously. They're not used to dealing with women, especially young ones like you."

A week later, she got a letter in the post.

"DEAR MISS LOVETT,

We understand from our agent, that you have been making enquiries about a leaky boiler. When you took the property on and signed the lease you did so on the understanding that the property was let to you at a reduced rent, due to this being a start up business. We understand that you have made certain changes to the property, without gaining our consent and this may affect your tenancy.

We will be sending our representative to the premises on Monday 17th March at 10.30am. Please ensure that you are on the premises at that time.

Simon Smith. Director.

Bold, Smith and Bold Property Agency."

"OH DAD, what am I going to do. Do you think they'll be cross that I've painted the place. And put up all those shelves. And got the vinyl laid?"

"Oh no, I don't think so love. After all you've improved the value of their investment. No, I'm sure once they see how nice you've made it look they'll be happy to replace the boiler. You need a good supply of hot water."

BY THE TIME Monday morning came round Elsie wasn't too worried. Her dad was right. They had done a great job smartening up the old place.

"WELL MISS LOVETT, I can see you've made this place your own. Very pink."

The way he said it was not complimentary.

"The agency is a little concerned that perhaps a beauty parlour is not the best thing for this prime real estate."

"But they knew what I was going to use it for before they let me sign the contract."

"Well of course my dear, it is rather unusual to have a woman running a business, especially a pretty young woman like you."

There was something about the way he said young and pretty that made her uneasy.

"I daresay I can reassure them that you are a suitable tenant, but you might need to do something for me, show me what exactly this little parlour of yours offers."

"Umm, what did you have in mind? We only do facials and manicures really. Oh and head massages."

"I thought you advertised all kinds of massages. Surely that's what beauty parlours do? Show me what skills you have. I have a lot of influence in this town. I can make or break a business you know. I thought you had staff? Surely you don't run this place all on your own, that's not a very good business model?"

"Oh no, Molly my assistant has just popped out to the whole-salers to get us some more massage oils, we had a run on them at the weekend. We're usually pretty quiet on Monday mornings, so it's a good time to catch up with all our admin stuff."

WHEN MOLLY RETURNED AN HOUR LATER, she was shocked to see Elsie curled up on one of the sofas, clutching a mug of tea. It was obvious she had been crying.

"Oh Elsie, whatever's wrong. Are you alright?"

It took a while for her to calm down.

"Oh Molly, it was so awful. That man from the agency said that I wasn't sticking to the terms of my lease. He said I shouldn't have done all that painting and made holes in the walls for the shelving, without the landlords consent. He said that they weren't aware I was so young and inexperienced and if they had known, they might not have let me have the shop."

She sniffed loudly and grabbed a pile of tissues from the box Molly had placed in front of her.

"So did he agree to replace the boiler? Surely that was the purpose of the visit."

"I'm not sure. I think so. He seemed happy enough when he left."

"But why are you crying, did he say something else? Or do something to you? Why was the CLOSED sign on the front door when I came back?"

The truth came out slowly, tears pouring down Elsie's face as she spoke.

"He said I had to show him what skills I had and demanded a massage. He said I should lock the door to make sure we weren't disturbed. I felt really uncomfortable but didn't see I had much choice. I was just hoping you'd be back quickly. Anyway I started

giving him a head massage. It was horrible, he didn't have much hair, so I was rubbing his bald pink scalp, trying to think of something else. Then he said it was too hot, so he stood up and took off his suit jacket. I did notice what nice quality it was: grey pinstripe fabric with a fancy label: Simpsons of Piccadilly. Must have cost a pretty penny.

I massaged his head, then he said he wanted his hands done too.

All the time I was touching him I was trying to concentrate on his white silk shirt and flashy red bow tie."

"But I don't understand why you're so upset? Did he do something else? Or say something inappropriate?"

She started to cry again.

"He kept wriggling, then said he wanted the full package. I said I didn't understand and he said that was nonsense, of course I must know what people expected at a massage parlour. He knew that I'd worked in Brighton. I don't know how he knew that though. He said if I was a proper masseuse I would give him the full works. And he threatened that if I didn't he would have to tell the landlord that I was running an irregular business and that my lease would be withdrawn."

"Oh Elsie, so did you do what he wanted?"

"No of course I didn't. What do you take me for? I wouldn't even do that to a boy I fancied, let alone a dirty old man like that. Anyway he went off in a huff, so I don't know what'll happen now."

The letter terminating her lease came a few weeks later. Apparently the landlord had reconsidered and decided his premises weren't actually suitable for use as a beauty salon after all and that she would have to leave within 30 days.

She tried to fight it, her dad and brothers were furious.

They tried phoning the landlord and even sent a solicitors letter pleading her case, but to no avail.

Elsie's beauty parlour closed its doors for the final time at the end of April, just before the summer season started. A few weeks later, as she did her usual morning walk along the seafront, she was horrified to see a new shop sign going up over *her* door: a red and white striped pole with the words: QWIKCUT, Gentlemen's Barber.

She went into a decline for a while. All her hopes and dreams had gone up in smoke. She sent her brothers to have a haircut at QWIKCUT, her salon, and they reported back that it looked exactly the same inside. Apparently Simeon, the new owner, had a penchant for pink, so had decided to keep everything, even purchasing new pink and white striped towels to replace the original ones. It seemed that a new hot water boiler had been installed as her brothers said that the water in the sinks had been steaming hot. The new owner had confided in them how lucky he had been to get the premises. Apparently it had been rented previously by a flighty young woman who was running a disreputable massage parlour, so the landlord had been forced to evict her. This information was relayed in a loud voice to a crowded shop and Elsie's brothers had been furious. How dare people talk about their sister in that way. Spreading vicious untrue rumours.

A couple of months later Molly and Elsie were wandering aimlessly around the shops. They had both managed to pick up jobs in Brighton, driving there together every day, but their hearts weren't in it, they had both loved working in their hometown and being their own bosses.

Coming out of Marks and Spencers, Elsie suddenly gasped and went pale.

"Are you alright? Do you feel faint?"

"It's him Molly. That old bloke over there. That's the bloke from the agency. The one who came to the shop."

"Which bloke?"

"That one over there with a newspaper tucked under his arm. In the grey pin stripe suit. With the white shirt and red bow tie. I'd recognise him anywhere."

"Oh no, I think you're wrong Elsie. That can't be him. That's old Mr. Jones the bank manager. I know that cos I know Jimmy the bank messenger. Last time I went in to cash a cheque he pointed the manager out to me. Mind you, Jimmy doesn't like him much."

"It's definitely him. I'd recognise that suit and bow tie anywhere. And his horrible bald head and that moustache."

ELSIE'S DAD was a member of the Conservative Club so he made some discreet enquiries. Herbert Jones was not very well liked there, so it was easy to get people to talk. It seemed as though the bank manager had made many enemies.

"Oh yes, he's a nasty bit of work all right. Dresses up in that fancy suit and bow tie, but underneath it all he's rotten to the core."

"My mate used to live in Newhaven and knows him well. Apparently he was always a rotter. Broke a lot of hearts too and they reckon he's got a few bastards around the place. Shame for his wife, she's lovely that Vera. Don't know what she sees in him."

"They say he's in cahoots with some dodgy property developer. Someone from London who brought up all old Carlo Finches buildings for a song. I don't think the Finch family really wanted

to part with them, but some of the buildings were in bad disrepair and they couldn't afford to do all the work. Shame, cos old Carlo worked hard to build up his fortune. He'd be turning in his grave if he could see those places now. All that big talk about renovating them. Those developers have done nothing at all as far as I can see. They just put people in those places, charge them high rents, then let the walls fall apart around them. I think it's disgusting, benefitting from someone else's misery."

"I heard that they got a few cheap loans from the bank here in town, and that in exchange Herbert Jones has a share in their business. Not sure how true that is mind you, although I do know that he put his in-laws in some crummy flat on the seafront. Not that they lasted long there, they were both dead within a few months."

"I remember that. Their daughter Vera, Herberts wife, is a lovely woman. She was heartbroken at her dads funeral. He was a member here at the Con Club for years you know."

ELSIE LOVETT never got over the disappointment of losing her business. She realised that it was all down to one man: Herbert Jones, and she vowed that one day she would get her revenge. No matter how long it took, one day she would make him pay.

She went to his funeral, sitting at the back of the church with a smile on her face. At last he had got his comeuppance. She was delighted that he was dead.

24

PEREGRINE (BANK INSPECTOR)

Peregrine (known by his close friends as Perry) was a bank inspector.

He had started his banking career as a junior clerk, but due to his family connections he was whizzed through the ranks and by the age of 27 had become a bank inspector. This was a much desired role, something between an accountant and a policeman and it appealed to him much more than sitting behind a boring old desk every day.

He had grown up in a wealthy household, his father was the second son of an old banking family, a private bank established more than a hundred years, that catered only to the rich and influential. In time Perry would probably take on a role there, but for now he was happy making his own way, establishing himself in the banking world without relying on his own family. Of course the family name helped. Doors were opened to him that would have remained firmly shut if his surname was merely Smith or Jones. Personal connections and recommendations ensured that his moves within the bank were smooth and easy.

Unlike some of the boys he had been at Eton with, Peregrine was not a snob. In fact he much preferred the company of ordinary people, not people who had grown up with a silver spoon in their mouths. He was not like them, not willing to bide his time living off his trust fund until he either married a rich woman or his parents died. His brothers were doing just that and he rather despised them for it. They in turn thought he was quite mad, trading his comfortable existence and all the servants at his beck and call in their family home, for a one bedroomed flat in Brixton and a 9 to 5 job in the bank.

He didn't care what they thought. He was enjoying his new found freedom. After the confines of boarding school and his parents rigid lifestyle, he loved meeting new people every day. Ordinary people who worked hard for their living. Who had mortgages, old cars and children at the local primary school. People who had to save hard to afford a two week holiday at the seaside. People who were living real lives.

When it had first been suggested that he join the bank inspectors team he had been a little unsure. What did it actually entail? Was it something he would enjoy, or would he be better off staying put where he was, working in a small branch with a bunch of really nice people. People he could chat to about anything: politics, the state of the world, last night's tv programme, the price of a loaf of bread. He loved being part of their world, not just the rarified world he had grown up in.

Now, he was glad he had decided to become a bank inspector. It meant he didn't have the same day to day conversations with the same people as he had been used to as now he was travelling all over the country with a small team. Usually there were just six or seven of them working together, but if they went to a much larger branch they added a few more to the team.

Their role was to "*maintain the integrity of the banks financial system.*"

In reality this meant that they would descend on a bank branch, just before closing time, unannounced. They would then insist that everyone would stop working momentarily. The bank doors would be closed at exactly 3.30pm and their inspection would begin. They would shadow each cashier as they tallied up their days takings and check that all of the banks procedures were followed to the letter. Every staff member was interviewed in turn and no-one was allowed to leave the premises until they were certain all monies were correct.

It was an anxious time for every member of staff, but as they were almost all completely honest and conscientious in their work, they had nothing to fear.

Peregrine quite enjoyed the drama of their initial arrival. He and his colleagues would march into the bank, wearing identical dark navy suits with white shirts and black ties. He had never been quite sure of the significance of the black ties, but guessed it was just a subtle way of striking fear into people. One of them would linger by the front door until closing time, presumably to ensure that no dishonest clerk took fright and ran away. The rest would make their way to the security door, waiting to be admitted after demanding to speak to the manager. It was a tense time, particularly for the first hour or so, while they were establishing their power. And they did have power.

They were there to assess the branches financial health, to make sure there was no stealing, cheating or underhand dealings. They would evaluate the branches risk management practices and ensure that they were complying with regulations. They would check all the financial statements, deposits and loans, looking for problems or irregularities. They would check for money laundering, unapproved lending and other kinds of financial crime. In short, they wielded a considerable amount of power and if violations or weaknesses were discovered they could impose sanctions and corrective actions.

HE HAD BEEN LOOKING FORWARD to their Eastbourne inspection. It wasn't often he got to spend any time at the seaside. They were due to begin their inspection on a Wednesday afternoon, thus giving them two further days in the week if they should find anything amiss. Usually they were able to get everything done in a couple of days, so he was hoping to get a bit of time leftover to take a stroll on the beach or even get a beer in the bar at the end of the pier. He loved piers. When he was small, their nanny had taken him and his brothers to the Palace Pier at Brighton and he could still remember how exciting it was. The noisy slot machines in the arcade, the smell of hot dogs and candy floss. The salty sea air. She had been a lovely nanny. Quite young, probably only in her late twenties, a pretty girl who had treated the little boys under her charge with great care. They had all been sad when she left to get married and was replaced by old Mrs. Latchet, a rather sour faced woman who believed that children, especially noisy boys, should be seen and not heard, until they were bundled off to boarding school.

Anyway, now he was here, booked into the Grand Hotel

on the seafront (the bank believed in treating their inspectors well) and looking forward to a nice evening stroll along the promenade.

"Good afternoon Mr. Jones. My name is Peregrine Smyth, chief inspector."

"Good day inspector. We weren't expecting you. Wednesday is our busiest afternoon you know. All the local businesses come in getting their cash for staff wages. And I'm rather understaffed at the moment. Some of my best people are off sick."

Peregrine nodded.

"Of course I understand Mr. Jones. May I call you Herbert? We do realise that our presence can be unsettling, but we will endeavour to fade into the background and let you all get on with it as usual. We are only here to observe."

"Actually I would rather you didn't call me Herbert if you don't mind. I try to run a tight ship here and I find that too much familiarity is not good for staff morale. It is much easier to keep these peoples respect if they don't refer to me by my Christian name. I trust you understand."

Peregrine understood very well. This man reminded him of his own father, a man who ruled by fear and treated people quite abysmally, particularly people he felt were lesser than himself.

"I see Mr. Jones. Of course I understand. Now perhaps we can go into your office, I will need to take that over for the duration of our inspection. My colleagues will be using some of the clerks desks and of course are right now with your cashiers, overseeing the tallying up of today's takings."

Herberts face had gone a rather unflattering shade of red and his words came out in an angry torrent.

"My office, why do you need to work in my office? Surely you

*can manage with my secretary's desk in the room next door? She
can come in here and sit with me in the meantime."*

*"Sorry old chap. The regulations are quite clear. We must
inspect all areas of the branch and that includes your office. May I
suggest you pop into the room next door and I will call you when I
have any queries to discuss."*

Herbert looked as though he was about to explode, but
he realised he had no choice. This man's report could make
or break his career.

*"Very well. I shall be available as required. In the meantime,
can I get one of my staff to make you a cup of tea. Perhaps some
chocolate digestive biscuits to go with it?"*

The inspection went well enough and only took one and
a half days. Most of the regulations had been followed to the
letter, although going through the files Peregrine had found
a few anomalies. There seemed to be an unusual amount of
unsecured overdrafts and loans, almost all of them to
women. The Bank would often overlook these, after all it
was important to curry favour with local businessmen,
people who could bring additional influential people and
contacts to the branch and branch managers such as
Herbert were given a certain amount of discretion to give
these loans as they saw fit. But it was still unusual, even in
the 1980's to give loans to women, particularly young ones,
with little obvious security.

Still, the rest of the inspection went well and Peregrine
was forced to give the branch a clean bill of health. He
disliked Herbert Jones intensely, the man was an unpleasant,
arrogant buffoon, prancing around in his expensive grey
pinstripe suit and red bowtie. Apparently, according to the
female staff, who had been rather taken with some of the
young handsome male inspectors, their boss was always

dressed like that. According to the younger ones he was also *"a bit too handsy for my liking. None of us like being in his office alone."*

But that was all hearsay of course, nothing that Peregrine, in all good conscience could include in his report.

That evening, after strolling in the moonlight along the seafront, he decided to pop into the hotel bar for a brandy, before retiring for the night. The other inspectors had all checked out, delighted to have finished their work so early, anxious to return home to their wives and children. Peregrine, having neither of these things, no wife and no children, had decided to stay on another night and was looking forward to a relaxing day sitting on the beach before returning to Brixton.

He was surprised to see Herbert Jones sitting at the bar with a very glamorous woman beside him.

"Good evening Mr. Jones. Glad to see you celebrating after getting a clean bill of health today. I know how traumatic these inspections are for everyone. Good evening Mrs. Jones, how do you do. My name is Peregrine Smyth and I'm the rotter who put your husband and his staff through the wringer today."

"Oh hello. I'm not Mrs Jones. My name is Brenda. I run the Leg of Mutton pub. Opposite the bank, you might have noticed us. I would have given you a nice discount if you'd popped in there for your lunch."

Herbert looked as if he wanted the earth to swallow him up, but quickly managed to recover his equilibrium.

"Oh yes, Brenda and I were just discussing a bit of business, so I thought it would be nicer to do it here, in this nice quiet bar, rather than some place in town where everyone will overhear."

Peregrine refrained from asking why such business couldn't be carried out in the bank.

The next morning, as he was sitting in the dining room finishing his toast and marmalade, he looked up to see the pair exchanging a long lingering kiss in the empty hallway. They obviously didn't realise they could be seen. They had also obviously spent the night there, as both were wearing the exact same clothes as they had the previous evening. Of course Herbert would have been unaware that the bank inspectors were staying there, otherwise he would surely have held his romantic night elsewhere.

Peregrine could feel his blood boiling. Infidelity was one of his absolute pet hates. His father had cheated on his mother endlessly. He could still remember how she had wept every time she found out about yet another of his women. Her cries had echoed around the whole house. When he was 14, she had finally had enough and after confronting her husband about his latest affair, she had gone into the horses stables and hung herself from a beam. His father had remarried just six months later, giving him a step-mother only a dozen years older than himself.

In that moment Peregrine hated Herbert Jones. He also hated his father and all the other men who treated their wives so abominably. It was unforgivable. Men like that didn't deserve to be happy, in fact sometimes he thought they didn't deserve to be alive at all.

25

———

SIMEON (BARBER)

Simeon couldn't believe his luck. He had always fantasised about owning his own barbers shop. For as long as he could remember, cutting hair had been his passion. As a little boy, he had persuaded his two sisters to let them practise his skills on their dolls, with the result that said dolls ended up with cute bob cuts, long ringlet curls and even a very short pixie cut one time, which made his sister cry. He hadn't realised that dolls hair wouldn't grow back like human hair, so he had to live with the shame of that mistake all the time he lived at home with his family. The doll would often be brought out and shown to visitors, partly in pride at his obvious talent, but also to shame him into leaving his sisters toys alone. Nothing distracted him from his passion though and at the age of 16 he signed up to do a hairdressing apprenticeship at one of the largest salons in Brighton. He was the most junior of junior apprentices there, his only tasks being to sweep up hair and make endless cups of tea for the wealthy clientele.

But he was very well liked by both clients and his

colleagues alike. He was a handsome boy, tall and slim with golden curls, some said he looked almost angelic. He was gentle and quietly spoken and when not in his standard work uniform of black t-shirt and black jeans (both of which set off his blonde looks to perfection) he dressed rather outrageously. His absolute favourite outfit and the one he often chose to wear on nights out, was a pink shirt, pink tight-fitting jeans, a yellow jumper slung casually around his shoulders and mustard colour suede loafer shoes. By the time he turned 18, his final year as an apprentice, he was well known around the town. Well known and well liked.

Simeon had lots of friends. Some were as colourful as him, some much quieter and more soberly dressed. But they all had one thing in common. They all preferred the company of other men. Brighton was the perfect place for them to live, as no-one commented on their sexuality or their flamboyant dress sense.

He was blissfully happy there. He still lived at home with his parents and sisters of course, he couldn't yet afford to rent a place of his own. That would happen in the next couple of years though. Once he was a fully fledged hair-dresser he intended to save as much as he could and put down a deposit on a nice little flat. His dad told him that was a pie in the sky idea *"Don't be daft lad. People like us don't own their own homes. Why saddle yourself with a big mortgage for years, when you can just rent a place. I daresay some of those rich mates of yours would be happy to rent you a room when you're ready."*

Simeons dad had known his son was gay since he was 13. He had always had his suspicions, most young boys didn't want to spend all their time styling their sisters dolls hair or choosing which outfits they should wear. As his children grew, he noticed that the girls always asked their brothers opinion about their clothes and asked him to accompany them on shopping trips.

He had struggled at first. He was a builder by trade, had been all his life, so worked with men who wolf whistled at girls and made derogatory comments about men they viewed as effeminate. To discover that his own son, his only son, preferred men, came as a dreadful blow to him. He grieved for a while. It was now the 1980's and the 1967 Sexual Offences Act had decriminalised male homosexual activity for consenting adults in private, but there was still an awful lot of stigma around. Simeon's dad knew that the police were clamping down on gay clubs in the town and unfortunately the AIDS epidemic was making people even more wary of anyone who was a little different. He knew that his son, a boy who had grown up on one of the roughest council estates in Brighton, now spent his free time frequenting these places.

The boy who had once roamed the antique shops in The Lanes, fished off the Palace Pier and delighted in sitting on green and white striped deckchairs on the pebbly beach, now preferred to dress outrageously (in his father's opinion), wear mascara, and attend endless parties.

"COME ON SIM, it'll be fun. You know how those rich old blokes like us pretty boys. They can't have us of course, but they like pretending their money will buy our favours."

HIS FRIEND SPOKE with a bitter edge. He was 45 years old and had known much heartbreak because of his sexuality. He was still good looking, but knew he was getting past his best, so he enjoyed hanging out with Simeon, his young colleague from the salon. It made him feel young again standing alongside the golden boy.

At one such party, held in the exclusive Grand Hotel on the seafront, Simeon met Herbert Henry Jones.

It was the usual boring party. Rich men and women stood in groups, gossiping and flaunting their wealth. They discussed the state of the housing market and how it was affecting their property portfolio. They discussed the latest car models, keen to let everyone know what their wealth was able to purchase. The women all wore the latest designer dresses and the men wore suits from the best tailors in the West End. Most of the guests were heterosexual, but loved to boast to their London friends that they had *"spent Saturday evening with some charming, interesting people in Brighton."*

"Sim, let me introduce you to Mr. Herbert Jones. He used to be my bank manager when I lived in Seaford. How are you Mr. Jones? Is life treating you well? How is that charming wife of yours? Vera wasn't it?"

The three men chatted for a while and Herbert said he would pop into the salon sometime for a haircut.

A week later he did and he insisted on being attended to by Simeon.

. . .

"*I was most impressed by our chat the other day. It seems you are very well thought of. And so handsome too.*"

Simeon didn't know what to say. He was used to being chatted up of course: with his angelic looks both men and women found him attractive. But this bloke was a bit strange, there was something odd about him.

"*I have a proposition for you.*"

He gripped the scissors more tightly in his hand and felt the cold steel against his skin.

How dare this old bloke come to his place of work and start chatting him up?

"*Oh relax old chap. I don't fancy you, I'm just here to offer you the chance of a lifetime.*"

Simeon relaxed.

"*I have a vacant premises in Eastbourne, right on the seafront, that would make an excellent barbers shop. It's right opposite the pier and I'm looking for an ambitious young man to run it. What do you think?*"

Simeon didn't know what to say. It had always been his dream to have his own place, but Eastbourne? Wasn't that where old people went to die? It certainly wasn't as lively as Brighton.

. . .

But Herbert was very persuasive and a few weeks later he found himself saying goodbye to all his friends and clients in Brighton and moving 22 miles along the coast to his new home.

The excitement of finally getting his own place almost made up for the disappointment of the night life in Eastbourne. It was very sedate in comparison. But he soon built up a regular clientele of people willing to pay a little extra to have their hair cut by such a talented man. Although it was technically a barbers shop, he was very happy to also have female clients. Several women followed him to the new place and eagerly told all their friends about him. *"Darling you absolutely must go to this new place. It's called QWIKCUT, a rather vulgar name I know, the darling sweet young man who owns it looks like an angel and has magic scissors. You won't be disappointed I promise."*

So, after a few months his business was flourishing and at least he could still pop back to Brighton whenever he wanted to, every weekend if he felt like it.

Life was good, apart from his dealings with Herbert Jones. The wretched man seemed to pop in every other week on the pretence of something or other and always demanded a haircut or shave while he was there.

Simeon began to dislike him intensely. On the surface the man was charming, well dressed and polite. Simeon particularly approved of the way he dressed. Rather conservative in his boring grey pin stripe suits (although they were beautifully cut and obviously expensive) but saved from being utterly dreadful by the flamboyant red silk bow ties he always wore. Simeon decided that one day, in the distant future, he too would make bow ties his trademark, although of course his would be rather more flamboyant and interesting than the ones Herbert wore.

The reason he came to dislike Herbert so much was partly the way he spoke down to people, the man was terribly arrogant. But there was also an underlying current of prejudice. Prejudice against anyone who the bank manager considered to be lesser than himself. Sitting in the barber's chair he would rant endlessly: *"Those damn youngsters have no standards, they drink beer, smoke and throw their rubbish around on our seafront. And as for those girls who insist on going out wearing next to nothing, then wonder why men look at them. The girl who had this place before you was a bit like that. Acted like she was a lady. Had to get rid of her in the end. Giving this place a bad name she was."*

Simeon was intrigued. He had heard a bit of gossip about the previous tenant and wondered how much was true. Over the years he had got used to malicious gossip, had often been the subject of it and knew just how harmful it could be.

He made enquiries. He had become good friends with several of the local shopkeepers, particularly Tony and Maria Finch from the Italian restaurant next door.

"That man is the scum of the earth. He ruins peoples lives. Don't get too involved with him Simeon. It won't end well."

He had been surprised at Maria's bitter tone.

"No, I mean it Simeon. That man drives people to their graves."

She was reluctant to say any more. She had kept her dead sisters secret all these years and didn't intend letting it out now, but she was desperate to stop this lovely young man getting hurt. She had seen the damage Herbert had done to Elsie, the girl who previously owned the salon.

He was intrigued. So perhaps he hadn't been so wrong in

his opinion of Herbert Jones. Maybe the man was a monster after all?

He made discreet enquiries, gently questioning everyone he met. He was surprised at the level of animosity he uncovered. It seemed that the bank manager was not such a respectable person as he professed to be.

He had been running his barbers for five years on the day it all changed. He had always paid his rent on time and had learnt not to complain about the gradual dilapidation of the building. Of course it was old, but surely the landlord was responsible for general maintenance, things like leaky roofs and unsafe power sockets? But every time he had mentioned such things over the years Herbert had become enraged, telling him he was lucky to have been given the opportunity to rent the place at all. Herbert said that the absent landlord, a property developer friend of his, had been most reluctant to accept him as a tenant, until the bank manager vouched for him personally. So he had learnt to keep his mouth shut, to pay for incidental repairs himself, without bothering the landlord. Luckily his business was a huge success, his reputation was stellar and people travelled far and wide for his magic scissors. It helped of course that his prices were far cheaper than the big salons of Brighton and London.

"Now my dear chap, I'm afraid we have to have a small rent increase. A bit more than last years. There have been a lot of extra expenses."

Simeon bristled. The only extra expenses were ones he himself had paid for. He had not asked the landlord for anything.

"I know how busy you are these days, so you can easily afford

it. I've told the landlord to expect the increase in next month's bank payment."

Simeon went pale. The figure quoted was more than twice what he was already paying. There was no way he could afford to pay that much, however successful the salon was.

He argued, but Herbert refused to budge. He tried appealing to his better nature, but realised that the man obviously didn't have one.

In the end he had no choice but to agree.

HE STRUGGLED FOR SIX MONTHS, getting more and more frustrated. Every day became a challenge. Would he get enough clients to cover the rent that week? His dream quickly became his nightmare and still Herbert turned up once a fortnight to demand a haircut and shave.

Holding the cut throat razor, about to trim up the bank managers bushy moustache, he suddenly had a vision of moving his hand and accidentally cutting the wretched man's throat. He didn't of course, it would have been too obvious and he would have been carted off to prison, which would break his father and sisters hearts. But he really wanted to.

A few days later he heard that Herbert had died. Frozen to death. And he rejoiced. That dreadful man would never hurt anyone again.

26

FOND FAREWELLS

"*Oh Vera, I can't believe you've decided to move, we're really going to miss you.*"

"*Oh love you'll still be able to pop in and see me, I'm only going to that nice retirement village down by the new marina. It'll be easy for you to call in there on your way home from work anytime you feel like it.*"

"*But what about all your stuff? You'll never fit it all into that place?*"

"*Oh I know that love and I've decided that I'll leave most of it here for the new people. If they don't want it they can always sell it, send it to the charity shop or take it to the tip. I'm just going to take the things I really love. And I'm going to treat myself to new furniture. Our shop is having a big closing down sale, so what with that and my staff discount, I can easily afford some lovely new things. I've got my eye on a pale green leather sofa and a couple of matching recliners. And some Scandinavian light oak bookshelves and coffee tables. I've already chosen some pretty green and white fabric to make curtains and cushions. And I'm buying a new bed.*"

"Oh Vera that sounds lovely. You sound really happy, I'm so pleased. You deserve some happiness after the dreadful year you've had."

"Thank you love." She sounded a bit choked up. It had been such a long time since anyone cared about her happiness.

JUST THREE MONTHS later Vera closed the front door of her childhood home for the last time. She could hardly believe that she was really *doing it. Moving out of the home where she had lived for her whole life. Fifty five years in the same place. A place she had expected to die in. But Herbert's death had changed all that.*

"OH VERA, I don't know what to say. You have been so kind to us. I still can't believe this is our house now. I can't believe you sold it to us for such a cheap price. I never thought I'd own a house like this. Ian and I thought if we worked really hard for a few more years, living with my mum and dad and saving every penny we could, that one day we might be able to afford a grotty flat. Never in my wildest dreams did I think we'd have a house like this, a house we could stay in forever and raise a family in."

"That's exactly what I want for you Betty, a happy home with children running around. It never happened for me, but I'm sure it will for you. Then I will be able to come and visit you and your babies here. And please promise me you'll make as many changes as you like, I realise the old place has got a bit shabby. Herbert just didn't like spending any money on it, said it was perfectly fine as it was."

There was a catch in her voice as she spoke.

"Of course Herberts nephews were jolly cross when I said I was selling it to you. I think they expected me to let them have it a cheap price. But they've already had their inheritance, they don't need anymore. They're just being greedy. And neither of them have bothered to come and visit me much since Herbert died. Just a couple of duty calls. They don't care about me at all. Not like you do Betty. I don't know what I would have done the last year, without you popping in twice a week to check up on me."

"Oh Vera, we will really take care of it. We'll give it a lick of paint to brighten it up. We might even paint over some of that dark wood furniture until we can afford to buy new stuff. It's very trendy now to paint furniture you know, all the designers on telly are doing it. But I'm never going to change your kitchen. I will always think of you whenever I sit in that lovely yellow room. And thank you so much for leaving me all your yellow bone china. I will treasure it."

Betty sounded close to tears too.

"Oh love, you're so welcome. You've been such a good friend to me. Since Herbert died I don't know what I would have done without your visits. Especially since I got made redundant from my job. That was such a blow, I suppose I thought the store would go on forever. But it's getting a bit past it's best now, time for us all to move on to pastures new I think."

Vera had been shocked to hear that Bobby's department store, the place she had worked at for almost 40 years, was going to close down. She knew the business had been struggling in recent years, people didn't seem to like the rather old fashioned department stores any more. So many of them were being forced to close down. But perhaps it was time she thought about retiring anyway. It was hard standing on her feet all day and financially she didn't need the money. She owned the house outright, Herbert's life insurance policy had paid the mortgage off and she had a very generous widows pension from the bank. In addition she had discovered that her late husband had been very canny with his money. He had earned an excellent salary and according to his accountant he had invested most of it in property over the years. This had come as a huge surprise to Vera. Herbert has always told her they had to be frugal: that his salary barely covered their expenses and that she was responsible for all the food bills and the gas and electricity. She had accepted this without question. After all, he was a bank manager and could surely be trusted to manage their affairs.

In fact it seemed that Herbert had managed *his affairs* very well. He had ensured there was always sufficient money to fund *his* desires: his expensive suits and flashy cars, his business trips and illicit affairs. He had even cheated her own parents, insisting on paying them far less than their house, her childhood home, was worth. All the extra money he had stashed away, all the properties he had bought, even the house and the car were in his sole name. Nothing, absolutely nothing was registered to her. She now realised that if he had chosen to leave her, she would have been left with virtually nothing.

VERA SMILED to herself as she turned the key in the lock for the last time. She spun around and handed the key to the young woman standing beside her on the doorstep.

"Now Betty love. You enjoy the place. I know you're going to be very happy here. As happy as I once was. I promise to come and visit as soon as I get back from my little trip."

.   .   .

SHE HUGGED Betty and stepped into the waiting taxi, tears in her eyes.

"OFF TO THE STATION LOVE? Are you going somewhere nice?"

The taxi driver spoke kindly. He had seen how upset she was.

"OH YES, I'm going to France. To Provence actually. I've always wanted to go there. To see the lavender farms. I love lavender."

VERA JONES SUNK back into the comfort of the leather taxi seat. She couldn't wait to get there. She had been going to evening classes for the last year to learn French: she so wanted to experience everything the country had to offer. She had rented a little villa for the whole summer. It looked lovely in the brochure: full of light coloured furniture, bright cushions and rugs. Colourful paintings by local artists hung on the walls and there were vases of fresh flowers every-where, in every room of the house. There was even a little garden full of herbs and flowers and a small swimming pool. The stone villa was situated right in the middle of an ancient market town, so every Saturday morning she planned to join the locals, walking there with her wicker basket slung over her arm, just like all the French ladies. And when she finally got back to Eastbourne, when the summer was over, she would move into her little apartment by the marina.

· · ·

SOME PEOPLE, on hearing her plans, had said what a shame it was that Herbert had died unexpectedly and couldn't join her on this adventure. She hoped they hadn't seen the look on her face. Going to France, or even moving to a brand new apartment at the marina, would never have been something Herbert would have agreed to. But now she didn't have to please him anymore. Those days were over. Those days when she had been a loving dutiful wife were gone.

OF COURSE she had never meant to kill him. The thought had crossed her mind many times over the years, but she would never have carried it out, however much he provoked her. Her friend Sarah always said she was a saint *"I don't know how you tolerate him Vera love. If he was my husband I'd have sent him packing years ago. Or wrung his neck."*

But that night her patience had snapped.

She had been on her girls night out with Sarah: the one night every month when she took time for herself. Herbert always made a fuss on these days, said she was being selfish not rushing home from work to cook his tea as usual.

"I suppose I'll just have to fend for myself again" he had muttered as he walked out of the door that morning, after consuming the hearty full English breakfast she had prepared for him. These days he didn't even bother to say anything remotely affectionate or give her a goodbye kiss. She was well aware that he gave his affections elsewhere. She had known for years that he probably wasn't faithful, but he covered his tracks well and she was never able to prove it.

. . .

THAT FATEFUL NIGHT she was driving home after a lovely Italian meal at Maria Finches place and a visit to the cinema to watch some old black and white crime movies. Every year, for the last three years, the local Business Association had put on a special Culture Week: showcasing travel, movies and dance and she had loved it. Herbert of course refused to go to any of the events with her, culture was absolutely not his kind of thing. Instead he preferred to drink at his local pub: The Twitch Arms.

THAT NIGHT he had got very drunk and was staggering home after having a huge row with Cynthia, the pub landlady. He and Cynthia had been having an affair for years and he had always promised to leave his wife and move in with her. That night, after all the other customers had gone, he had hung around, expecting to be invited upstairs as usual. But Cynthia had had enough of his idle promises. They had had a huge row standing in the pub doorway and unfortunately Vera had driven past at that very moment. He didn't see her of course, he was too busy trying to caress Cynthia.

VERA HAD DRIVEN her little car slowly away, tears pouring down her face. It was the first time she had real proof of his philandering and it hurt terribly. All the years she had been a good loyal wife, all the things she had given up to make him happy. How stupid had she been?

As she turned the corner into the lane behind their house she could see him staggering along. He had obviously drunk an awful lot. Hopefully he would choose to sleep in the spare room tonight. She wasn't sure if she could face him yet. Maybe she'd know what to do in the morning?

She slowed down and watched him wobble from side to side and then something told her to speed up, to get rid of him once and for all. She put her foot on the accelerator. Her headlights were on full beam. She wanted him to see.

She was only a few yards away when she came to her senses and put her foot on the brake. What on earth was she doing?

Unfortunately she didn't brake in time and there was a gentle thump as the car hit him. It barely touched him, but in his drunken state, it was enough to make him lose his balance and fall backwards onto the hard concrete path.

She reversed the car and watched in horror as he tried to stand up. But there was nothing for him to grab onto and he fell over again.

Satisfied that there was no blood and that she obviously hadn't killed him, she reversed the car and drove around the corner, parking in front of their house. She went indoors, made a cup of tea to settle her nerves and took it up to bed. He would obviously be furious when he came in. She didn't think he had realised it was *her* car, it had been very dark in the lane and he was far too drunk to think properly. She would have to deal with it in the morning when he had sobered up.

Of course he never came home. Instead he lay on the path and froze to death, completely covered in a thick layer of snow.

Although she had been shocked, she had no regrets. He had been a rotten husband, cruel and unkind and she was so much better off without him. She was sorry that poor Betty had discovered him like that though. It must have been such an awful shock to discover his dead frozen body, but at least she had been able to give the girl her house at a cheap price. That made her feel better, a bit less guilty.

Now she was free to live her own life at last.

She couldn't even pretend she was sorry he was dead. And *technically* she hadn't really killed him, she had just left him there to die. Everyone knew it had been a silly accident.

The End.

DID YOU ENJOY THIS BOOK?

Please leave me a review!

Your feedback is important to me; please leave a review wherever you purchased this book, or meet me on my website: www.patbackley.com

I look forward to hearing from you!

ABOUT THE AUTHOR

Pat Backley is an English woman, who decided at the age of 59 to become a Kiwi. She now lives in Auckland, New Zealand.

She published her first book just before her 70th birthday and having discovered her passion, she now intends to write until she dies! Pat also loves to travel, garden, read, walk on the beach and socialise.

She has lived a colourful and interesting life, loves people, places and architecture and her books reflect these passions.

Her other works include:

Daisy; *The Second Daisy*; *From There To Here, With An Awful Lot In Between*; *Seventy Years Worth Of Travel*; *The Abandoned Wives Handbook*

ANCESTORS SERIES: *Valentine George, Lou And Eustace, Dot And Ben*

She has also contributed articles and short stories to magazines and anthologies, including *The Warrior Women Project*, *Relatable Voices*, and several charity anthologies for *Ages Of Pages*, raising money for Duffy Books In Homes.